NATURE'S SHIFT

Borgo Press Fiction by BRIAN STABLEFORD

NATURE'S SHIFT

A TALE OF THE BIOTECH REVOLUTION

BRIAN STABLEFORD

THE BORGO PRESS

MMXI

AUTHOR'S NOTE

This novel is loosely based on a short story entitled "The Growth of the House of Usher," which first appeared in *Interzone* 24 in 1988.

NATURE'S SHIFT

Published by Wildside Press LLC

www.wildsidebooks.com

DEDICATION

For Linda

CONTENTS

But from the first 'twas Peter's drift
To be a kind of moral eunuch,
He touched the hem of Nature's shift
Felt faint—and never dared uplift
The closest, all-concealing tunic.

Percy Bysshe Shelley, "Peter Bell the Third"

CHAPTER ONE

I didn't want to go to the funeral. I told myself repeatedly, while I waited for the trains that took me from Lancaster to Birmingham, Birmingham to Bristol, and from Bristol to Exeter, that I would do better to turn around and go home, and avoid any reconnection with the desolate past. I told myself again when I caught my first glance of the Crystal Palaces of Eden and the Great Pyramid in the distance. I couldn't help feeling a twinge of nostalgia, of course, but any affection I had for the place, and the memories associated with it, was drowned by the residue of disappointment it had left behind, and the aching wreckage of…well, calling it a broken heart would probably be stretching cliché too far.

I was still telling myself that I shouldn't have come when I was confronted by the huge gates of Eden, far more steely than pearly. They were manned by uniformed security guards, and when I told one of them my name I had a faint, absurd flash of hoping that he might consult a list on his phone or a virtual palm-print, decide that I wasn't on it, and turn me away.

The fact that he didn't have to consult his phone or the palm of his hand seemed somehow ominous, although it was presumably just a tribute to technical elegance. I didn't suppose that the poor fellow had been required to memorize two hundred names—there were more than four hundred people at the ceremony, but they included a lot of family groups—so I concluded that he had some kind of subtle earpiece relaying information to him from a central control-room, whose guardians obviously had eyes as well as ears on me.

At any rate, the petty Saint Peter didn't turn poor Sinner Peter away, or even ask to see any kind of documentation. I didn't have an invitation, as such—but someone, presumably Rosalind, had taken the trouble to send me a notification of the time and place of the funeral, not via the web but by means of a courier-delivered black-rimmed card. I had it in my pocket, just in case. Would I have had the courage to refrain from showing it, if I had been asked, in order to be turned away? Probably not. I had come at the way from Lancaster, after all, even though I knew, deep down, that I shouldn't have.

I mustn't exaggerate, though. It wasn't a case of fascination, like those old myths about birds hypnotized by snakes. I was there because I needed to be there, even though I knew I shouldn't want to. I needed to see Rowland again. I needed to give him my sincere condolences. It never occurred to me for an instant that he wouldn't be present at his own sister's funeral—and not just any sister, but Magdalen. That was beyond belief, even for Rowland.

If I'd known that he wouldn't be there, I probably wouldn't have gone—not because of any disrespect for Magdalen, with whom I had once been in love, or even because the thought of having to face Rosalind without any protective presence to shield me from her glare was too much to bear, but simply because Rowland's absence would have made the whole occasion seem pointless. It was almost as if, without Rowland there to bear witness, Magdalen couldn't possibly be dead, and the funeral couldn't possibly be taking place.

At any rate, I did want to see Rowland; that was the only reason I had for going back to Eden. We were still friends, in some mysterious sense independent of actual communication. Even if he did take invisibility to extraordinary lengths when it came to web-presence and web communication—to the extent that people who did not know him would have declared him a friendless recluse—I knew that there was something unbreakable and eternal in the bond we had forged in our late teens and early twenties. I hadn't seen him in the flesh since he had taken up residence thousands of miles away in Venezuela, in the most remote spot he could find—presumably in order to get away from Rosalind, although that bond too was eternal and unbreakable—and it was at least seven years since I'd spoken to him over the phone, but the omission was a result of careless neglect, not design.

I hadn't spoken to Magdalen either—in fact, I hadn't seen or spoken to Magdalen since she'd left Venezuela to return home, after not much more than a year in the tropics. It wouldn't have surprised me very much to learn that Rowland hadn't spoken to Magdalen for years either, in spite of the fact that their bond was the most intimate and intense of them all. If so, I imagined, as I crossed the threshold of Eden, he must be feeling bitterly regretful now.

Inevitably, I only recognized a tiny fraction of the people making their way along the pathways toward the purpose-built marquee where the ceremony was to be held. Everyone was on foot; although there was a driveway leading from the steely gates to the base of the Pyramid, all vehicles had been halted at the gate and diverted into an *ad hoc* car park. Today, Eden was for pedestrians only. There was no way of getting to the marquee without smelling the flowers, save for donning a gas mask.

You can get very unobtrusive gas masks nowadays—bimolecular films that are as invisible as a recluse's web-presence—but it would have been impolite to wear one to a funeral. Even though I didn't recognize ninety-five per cent of the mourners, and only knew most of the rest from the TV, I didn't suppose for a moment that they included anyone impolite. After all, we all knew that there was nothing to fear in a crudely literal sense—that Rosalind had no wish to harm us. Subtle manipulation was, of course, a different matter. That was her deepest inclination as well as her chief stock-in-trade. When he was in a slightly vindictive mood, Rowland had been wont to remark that although God had almost equaled Rosalind's talent as a creator, he'd never shown anything like her ability as a control-freak. People with a sense of humor always laughed at that, assuming that he was making a slightly off-color joke. I never did. I'd actually met Rosalind, on several occasions, when Rowland and Magdalen had invited me to their exotic home, and had felt the awesome force of her personality.

Have the flower-beds been specially replanted for the occasion? I couldn't help wondering, as I walked between two that were gloriously in flower—even though it was April and the Met Office directors, ever sticklers for tradition, were keeping the weather cool and showery—*and if so, what effect are the flowers supposed to have?*

There was nothing gloomy about the visual aspect of the flowers, which were mostly in pastels shades of blue, yellow, purple and pink, without a lily to be seen, but Rosalind wasn't that unsubtle, except when she really wanted to be, and I knew that any kicker would be in the scents. Had Rosalind's research in psychotropics achieved sufficient sophistication to allow her to engineer flowers that would assist mourners to cultivate an appropriately mournful mood? Probably—but that would have been an insult of sorts. If the scents of Eden's flowers had been carefully planned for the occasion, according to her own aesthetic scheme, they would be sowing more complex emotions than mere sadness. When it came to moving in mysterious ways, God might still have the edge on Rosalind, but not by much.

This had been Roderick's Eden before it was Rosalind's however, so I didn't just look at the flowers. I searched for their pollinators, expecting bees—but what I actually found was black butterflies. As soon as I saw them, fluttering discreetly between the blooms, I kicked myself mentally for not having guessed. It was the perfect combination of delicacy and ostentation. Black butterflies: the perfect mutes to lead a funeral procession for one of Rosalind's daughters, one of the pillars of the Hive of Industry. Black bees couldn't have done the job nearly so well.

Before the Crash, I knew, there had been a species of butterfly called a Mourning Cloak, but its wings had not been black. The butterflies in Eden's specially-replanted beds were not a resurrected or simulated species; they were new. They were Magdelen's butterflies, made for her commemoration. If the Hive of Industry's marketing department decided that there was money to be made out of funeral butterflies, the ones supplied for future events would not be the same as these; Rosalind would make sure of that.

Even after I had seen and understood the significance of the butterflies, it took me at least three minutes to relax and breathe with some semblance of natural rhythm as I moved through the flowers-beds. The only olfactory sensations of which I was conscious were sweet, pleasant and welcoming—but the whole point of olfactory psychotropics is that they by-pass consciousness entirely and work at a deeper mental level, so I couldn't be certain, purely on the grounds of what I was feeling consciously, that there wasn't some subtler subconscious effect. The very uncertainty and confusion of my feelings seemed to be a guarantee of sorts that there was no insidious manipulation going on, and that the pleasant scents were exactly what they seemed, but....

I abandoned the vicious circularity of that train of thought.

They *were* pleasant scents, and not in any crude quasi-pheromonal sense. They might not have been calculated to make people feel sad, but any reference they were making to the ancestral olfactory spectrum was quite chaste; even their sweetness seemed strangely wholesome, although there isn't a lot of room for sophistication in that regard. On the other hand, if anyone were capable of discovering a new kind of sweetness, it would surely be Rosalind, or one of her daughters. Rosalind was not to be underestimated, in biotechnical terms, and nor were her daughters. She was, after all, the Queen Bee as well as the Bee Queen, and her surviving offspring were fearsome workers.

Even Magdalen had been a fearsome worker, in her way.

Not that Rowland was any sort of drone, of course, but he had always stuck out as something of an anomaly within the family, even if one contrived to set aside his sex. He wasn't by any means a fly in the ointment, but he wasn't a team player either. While his sisters worked with relentless determination on Rosalind's behalf, following the disciplined lines of Rosalind's imagination, Rowland had always been determined to exert his independence, not merely to do what Rosalind did not want to do, but, if possible—and it was a *very* big if—to do things that couldn't or shouldn't be done, in Rosalind's opinion. When I had first met him, I had assumed that it was a perfectly natural teenage rebellion against parental authority—with which I, of all people, had every reason to sympathize—but as I had got to know him better I had learned that it cut much deeper than that the usual generation-gap issues. I had sympathized with that, too.

Some of his more casual acquaintances had thought—and said—that he was merely taking after Rosalind, because she had taken a similar attitude to her father, but Rowland always denied that, and Magdalen had always backed him up. I had never had the privilege of meeting Roderick the Great myself—he had died many years before I met Rowland and Magdalen—so I had never had the opportunity to study Rosalind in the role of daughter, only that of matriarch.

I decided, on due reflection, that the scent of the flowers produced for the occasion couldn't have been loaded with psychotropics of any sort, because Rosalind would definitely have considered any ploy of that sort beneath her dignity. That didn't mean, however, that they couldn't intended to create a funereal mood by underhanded means, because Rosalind understood the placebo effect as well as anyone. The mere possibility that the flowers might be psychotropic, and might be intended to cultivate sadness, might lead some people actually to feel sadness. Sadness is only an emotion, after all, and in Rosalind's world-view, emotion was mostly illusion….

There was a threat of vicious circularity in that line of thought too, and I abandoned it.

In any case, there was no illusion at all in the gut-wrenching sadness that I felt as I approached the marquee, because I wasn't some client of the Hive putting on show of polite solidarity. In my case, there was no need for any artificial stimulus of any sort. I wasn't the only person who had loved Magdalen, by any means, but I had loved her best, and longest.

The general mood, as the crowd became more compact around the marquee, did seem decidedly solemn, though. Perhaps, I thought, even in a crowd almost entirely made up of people who did business with Rosalind rather than people who had known Magdalen personally, my grief might somehow be contagious—but that was sheer nonsense, and I tried to pull myself together.

The marquee wasn't any kind of standard model, of course. Funeral marquees are becoming rare nowadays—though not as rare as wedding marquees—because the conquest of death is making real progress, and rarity has inevitably bred originality as well as ostentation, but the majority of atheist funerals still retain the lessons of church architecture in attempting to cultivate an atmosphere of substituted sanctity. Add a crucifix or two and most of the structures in which early twenty-second century funeral ceremonies are held could still one mistaken for chapels or temples…but not the one that Rosalind had build for Magdalen.

Roderick the Great had been, among his many other talents, a gantzer of genius, and Rosalind hadn't forsaken that aspect of the family tradition while developing her own distinctive expertise. She was something of a Crystal Palace specialist, though— the Great Pyramid had been Roderick's—and she had obviously felt that she ought to stick to what she did best, especially, for her eldest daughter's funeral.

Magdalen's was, I presumed, the first family funeral Rosalind had ever had to organize. She had been too young to take a hand in planning Roderick's. In any case, the Great Man had surrounded himself with an entourage of organizers, and would probably have designed every last detail of his own funeral in advance, so that his actual death merely functioned as a trigger setting the mechanism in motion, leaving nothing for Rosalind to do but learn her own allotted bit part. How she must have hated that, even as a child! All of her other daughters were still alive, as was her one and only son.

The marquee was a dome of glass—a dome of many-colored glass, in fact. It was however, a plain dome, geometrically speaking, and its many colors retained a dutiful fidelity to the harmonics of the Newtonian spectrum. It was elegant and tasteful, if not obviously funereal at first glance. Some people might have mistaken its hemispherical smoothness and its insistent colors for an attempt to lighten the mood—a belated attempt to resurrect the twenty-first century vogue for pretending that funerals ought to be celebrations of life rather than defiant resentments of death—but Rosalind was the last person in the world to try to resurrect a vogue that was stupid as well as obsolete. She had nothing at all against resurrection, but she was a strict utilitarian in that regard. She had lived through the worst years of the Crash as a child and adolescent, and even though her view of it had been largely obtained from the top of Roderick's Great Pyramid, she knew what death was, and knew that it was not something to be met meekly, with eyes turned resolutely backwards.

To me, the statement made by the colored marquee was one of raging against the dying of the light—but I knew that I had to be careful of seeing it through the lens of my own imaginative inclinations. Rowland had often criticized me for "thinking in quotes," deeming the habit slavish. He was not an admirer of poetry himself, least of all Romantic poetry, and had not reacted well when I had once referred to him, intending to pay him a compliment, as a "tyger" burning bright in the forests of the night, although he had mercifully failed to understand when I had once addressed him in a slightly less complimentary mood, as "Manfred."

There are, I know from experience, terminological purists

who argue that glass-working is not, strictly speaking, gantzing, that label being—in their opinion—only applicable to processes of biological cementation that organize particulate matter. Because glass is a supercooled liquid rather than a agglomerated solid, the neobacteria responsible for its secretion and shaping have a distinctive biochemistry that is distinguished in several significant genomic and proteonomic ways from the kinds of gantzers that raise palaces from clay, granite or unrefined sand. I had never been that kind of purist, though, and had once taken a civil engineering course in company with Rowland, who thought that narrow definitions were almost as dangerous to mental flexibility as thinking in quotes. To our minds, the fact that "gantzing" was a derivative of a human surname rather than any kind of genetic terminology gave it a flexibility that fully entitled it to be applied to all kinds of modern building techniques, as laymen usually did. Leon Gantz had been a revolutionary, whose name was fully entitled to become legend and transcend pedantry; Roderick Usher's name might well have done likewise, had it not already been legendary, in an entirely different context.

That was why Roderick was usually known simply as Roderick, except when he was favored as Roderick the Great, and Rosalind simply as Rosalind, except when she was called the Queen Bee. The current House of Usher wanted nothing to do with a literary inheritance that was inseparable from the notion of falling, let alone the tacit notions of decadence and degeneracy.

I could sympathize with their attitude, even though the unfortunate literary implication of my own name was far too esoteric to qualify as legendary, and I wasn't entirely confident that my own existential trajectory was as diametrically opposed to the accidental precedent as the Ushers' was. Roderick and Rosalind were all about rising, resurrection and resistance to decay and degeneration: they were movers and shakers in the post-Crash restoration and revivification of the ecosphere, the legacy of the new Eden, and the conquest of death. As for Rowland...well, the jury was still out on that one. Rosalind was understandably disappointed in his refusal to work for the Hive, but I retained the loyal conviction that he too was a biotechnological creator of genius, destined to stimulate the course and cause of human progress.

The fact that Rowland had deliberately taken a flamboyantly independent course in his life and research, rather than following meekly in the tracks of his mother and grandfather, seemed to me to be essential to the prospect of his making an impact on the world. I thought that there was every reason to hope that the scope of his achievements would eventually turn out to be just as spectacular as those of his mother and grandfather. All three of them, at any rate, were firmly committed to the notion that upwards was the only way to go. In my view, though, the Earth is a sphere, and if you anchor your conceptual geometry to its center, every direction is up that leads to the light, and there's nowhere to fall at all: the worst case scenario is inertia, and contentment with the dark. That wasn't Rowland's style at all, no matter what uninformed observers might think of his retreat to the wilds of Venezuela and his long silence. He might have set his sights on stranger skies than the Hive's starry firmament, but they were definitely not earthbound.

That, at any rate, was what I thought as I made my way toward Magdalen's marquee, expecting to see him there, if not center stage, then as close to Rosalind as anyone would ever be permitted to get.

CHAPTER TWO

As I was still studying the colored dome from without, with what I hoped might pas for a connoisseur's eye, I finally caught a glimpse of someone I knew—who seemed distinctly relieved to catch sight of a familiar face. He hurried to meet me.

"Peter?" he said, as if he were uncertain as to the reliability of his memory. "Peter Bell?" He didn't add "the Third" because he hadn't known my father and grandfather, who had passed through the hallowed halls of Imperial College before his time— the time of his tenure, that is, not his life; he was considerably older than my father, and looked it. Even if he had overlapped with the time of my father's passage, he wouldn't have known him, because my father and I had studied different subjects.

I nodded my head, in case he really was in need of confirmation. "Professor Crowthorne," I said. I tried to remember exactly how long it had been since I'd seen him, and settled on nine years, a couple of years after my doctorate had been conferred. I also tried to remember his first name, although I didn't imagine that I'd need to use it, but I couldn't. His initials were J. V., but whether he was a John, a James, a Julius or a Justin I had no idea. He hadn't changed a bit—but that was hardly surprising. He hadn't attempted to make use of somatic engineering to restore any kind of travesty of his lost youth, but he had made use of active cosmetics to freeze his features at the apparent age of fifty. At a rough estimate, he must have been seventy-five, but I knew that he hadn't retired from research, or even from teaching.

"Have you seen Rowland?" was, inevitably, the professor's next question. He had been Rowland's personal tutor at Imperial, and Magdalen's too, though not mine. He only knew me as a participant in his seminars.

"Not yet," I told him. At that point in time, of course, I still expected to, although the fact that the professor hadn't seen him either did sound a slight semi-conscious alarm bell.

"I don't think any of the family have emerged from the Pyramid yet," Crowthone was quick to add. "I suppose I should have said, have you seen Rowland *recently?* I tried to keep in touch, but...these days, distance isn't supposed to matter any more, but Venezuela hasn't recovered from the Crash yet, has it? How could it, having lost ninety-five per cent of its peak population?"

"Things still seem to be pretty bad out there," I confirmed, although I only had the same newsfeeds to draw on as the professor.

One of the reasons why Rowland had moved to Venezuela was that it had one of the shorelines hit hardest by the ecocatastrophe. The delta region where he had taken up residence had been under the sea for more than a generation, and still suffered freak tides, as well as frequent hurricanes, on an irregular basis. It might have been feasible for the natives to begin building harbors again, but it would probably be another twenty years, at least, before any sort of local fishing industry became viable, and there were no custodians of that particular cultural tradition left in on the coast in question. Moving in had been a challenge even for someone with Rowland's inherited wealth and biotechnological abilities.

A bold gantzer was supposed to be able to erect buildings anywhere, but it had required something more than boldness to single out the Orinoco delta when Rowland had taken himself off there, and I doubted that he had a neighbor within two hundred miles, as yet, no matter how rapidly the nation's general reconstruction was proceeding in the west and along the Colombian border. The two great industries that had sustained the nation's economy, after a fashion, before the Crash—fossil oil and cocaine—were both as dead as the dodo. Genetic engineering had replaced them both, fossil oil with cane oil and kelp oil, and cocaine with a whole generation of stimulant drugs, by far the most fashionable of which was Aether. The surviving Venezuelans could only look with envious eyes at such neighbors as Trinidad and Brazil, which—for different reasons—had come through the collapse in much better economic shape.

"Not that I've seen anything more of Magdalen in recent years," Professor Crowthorne added. "You must have kept in touch with her?"

"I'm afraid not," I said. "We never really got back in touch, after she returned from Venezuela. I thought she might want to talk to me about it…about leaving Rowland behind, that is… and I kept expecting her to call, but somehow, it didn't seem appropriate for me to call her. Maybe we were both expecting the other to make the first move, both leaving it to the other— silly, I suppose. But I didn't feel that I could, in the circumstances, and months became years, and now…."

Now, it was too late, but I couldn't quite pronounce the words. The professor came to my rescue. "Time flies, alas," he said. "For everyone, of course—but especially for scientists, I think. The scientific mind has to be adept at concentration, dedicated in focus, inexhaustibly patient…and all of that easily becomes a matter of shutting other people out, a means of obsession." He sighed, then added: "A tragic business, this. Now that we're supposed to be able to live for hundreds of years…not that anyone's proven it yet…it seems a terrible shock when someone dies so young."

The cautionary interjection was typical of him. He had a more intense interest in the possibility that humans might now be able to live for hundreds of years, by courtesy of advanced internal technology, than most people, having been born into an era in which centenarians were exceedingly rare and the Crash was making certain that even the citizens of Fortress Britain had less than a fifty-fifty chance of reaching their natural lifespan. Had there not been such sweeping changes in his life-time, he might now be confronting the possibility of imminent death himself, but he had no way of knowing, at the dawn of the New Era, how long he might endure…or what new problems that endurance might throw up. His remark about the lack of proof wasn't just a reflection of his uneasy experiences during the tail end of the ecocatastrophe, though. He was by nature a cautious person, unprepared go take anything on trust that was as yet untested by time and experience.

Although I assumed that the primary reason for his refusal of any attempt to look younger had been the ridiculousness that most such cosmetic endeavors conferred on their victims, I suspected that Professor J. V. Crowthorne actually liked the venerable look, feeling that it was not only suited to his status as a university teacher but to his personality. Some people are born to peak at twenty-one, and every sign of aging they accumulate is an insult to their beautiful identity, but some are born to peak in advanced maturity, and moderate aging befits the image of their essential wisdom. He was one of the latter.

I was a university teacher myself too, now, but I calculated on keeping my youthful appearance for a long time yet, even though beauty was definitely not my strong suit. By the time I reached seventy—still more than thirty years in the future—I suspected that venerable would be completely out of fashion, even in science and politics.

I agreed with the professor that Magdalen's premature death was tragic, of course. I also agreed with his judgment that time flew, and his assessment of the proclivities of the scientific mind, but didn't bother to say so. I got the impression that he wanted to ask me whether I knew how Magdalen had died, but didn't dare, for fear of indelicacy. In fact, I didn't know, but I had the same inevitable suspicion that he did. When anyone dies young these days, unless they do it in public, as the victim of a traffic accident or some kind of sporting misadventure, the first question that springs to anyone's mind isn't *how* but *why*. When such a death isn't suicide, the actual cause tends to be boldly advertised, so as to set aside any possibility of misunderstanding. Even though Rosalind was a law unto herself, I couldn't imagine her allowing people to believe, by default, that Magdalen had killed herself, unless she actually had. If it had been some exotic disease or untreatable cancer—for such things are not yet extinct, by any means—the fact would surely have been published, but the web had been silent. The people who knew the cause of Magdalen's death were maintaining silence.

Which did not, of course, make her death any less tragic.

"I've never been here before," Professor Crowthorne said, deliberately looking away from the marquee at the Crystal Palaces, and meekly allowing his gaze to be trapped and drawn upwards by the mighty pyramid. "I arrived early, so I was able to have a quick look around. It's very impressive, isn't it?"

"Yes it is," I agreed. "I haven't been here in quite a while myself. The site has expanded since then, but this area is much the same. It was always impressive—as it was designed to be. I never met Roderick, but I know that he took his Greatness seriously. When he decided to found an Eden, he didn't just want to match the mythical one; he wanted to better it."

"He can hardly be blamed for having a sense of his own grandeur," the professor observed, as the crowd began to converge on the entrance to the marquee and we automatically moved with it, falling into step side-by-side like well-disciplined marionettes. "It wasn't a delusion. Even if he had only solved the bee problem...."

He left it there because he knew that he didn't have to go on. He might not have been entirely certain about my name, but he knew that I must have heard him explain that particular aspect of the "emergent ecocrisis" before, and shouldn't slip into lecturing mode now.

Solving "the bee problem" had only been the beginning of Roderick's great career. If it had been a unique problem, it wouldn't have been too difficult to solve. Natural selection might even have done the trick by itself, without the aid of genetic engineering, if civilization had had a hundred years to spare. Once genetic engineering had got into its stride in the early twenty-first century, the task of producing strains of bees that were immune to colony collapse disorder wasn't all that difficult, technically speaking. If Roderick Usher hadn't done it, other people would have filled the breach readily enough. In fact, though, "the bee problem" had only been a symptom of a more general malaise, and it was in tackling the many facets of the bigger problem that Roderick had truly demonstrated his greatness.

The ecosystemic connections between insect species, and between insects and the species above and below them in the food-chain, had been forged over tens of millions of years of evolution, in an environment that was constantly changing— but not at the pace suddenly inflicted on it by the rapid growth of human civilization, modern agriculture and an aggressive war launched against insect "pests" by humankind. In the early phases of that war, it hadn't been easy to distinguish insect friends from insect foes, and the secondary effects of specific assaults had been incalculable.

Fundamentally, the problem had been fairly simple, and offered several possible routes to potential solution. Many of the crops that humans relied on as primary producers, to feed themselves and their livestock, were pollinated by insects, a significant number of them by specialist pollinators like bees. When the specialists began to run into trouble, there were several ways that the problem could have been tackled. New primary producers could, in theory, have been selected, developed or designed. New ways of cultivating the existing primary producers, which freed them from dependency on insect pollinators, could, in theory, have been devised. The simplest and most straightforward approach was, however a matter of producing specialist pollinators that were immune to the particular trouble in question, either by modifying the existing specialists or producing substitutes, whether by selective breeding or direct genetic manipulation.

Roderick and his associates had mounted a two-pronged

assault on the problem, attempting to modify both the crop species and their specialist insect pollinators, in order to insulate both species from their ecosystemic environment, in what Roderick had labeled "dedicated symbiotic partnerships." He aimed to free the crops from all the non-human species that used them as nourishment—the pests—and also to free their loyal insect handmaidens from predation and parasitism, while making sure that the handmaidens' own nourishment was assured by the nectar of the species whose reproductive needs they served. He had set out to provide all the important food crops, one by one, with that kind of ecological insulation, and had made such rapid progress that, by the time Rosalind inherited his empire, there had been abundant scope for moving on, not merely to species used for food that were matters of gourmet delicacy rather than dietary staples, but to plant species that were economically significant for other reasons. Nowadays, the cutting edge of the Bee Queen's vast Hive of Industry had little to do with foodstuffs, and much more to do with such refinements of plant perfume as olfactory psychotropics.

"So what are you working on nowadays?" I asked Professor Crowthorne, taking the lead in the inevitable ritual exchange that marks every meeting between scholars, even though the answer, nine times out of ten, is: "still the same old stuff."

"Still the same old stuff," the professor replied. "Modifying tree species for the production of construction materials...not that there's much demand for specialist woods these days, given the ever-increasing versatility of neobacteria." He looked up as he spoke, at the fabric of the glass dome, which now arched above us like an artificial firmament, more varied and more orderly than Nature's sky.

"Wood will never go out of fashion," I assured him. "In fact, once the current housing revolution has run its course, with respect to gross structures, the pendulum of preoccupation is bound to swing back to matters of décor. Craftsmen love wood. They always will. Plastic is strictly utilitarian; wood carries forward the legacy of life. The day of your greatness will come,

Professor—never doubt it."

He blushed—not with embarrassment, because I was laying it on too thick, but with pleasure, because I was at least making the effort to pretend that I cared.

"What about you?" he said. "Still a plant man?" Obviously, he hadn't read any of my recent publications.

"Not exactly," I said. "I retreated down the evolutionary scale somewhat. Most of my practical work nowadays is with marine algae."

"Really?" he said. "That's presumably why you've retreated to the far north—for the sea coast." Lancaster wasn't exactly the "far" north, and Morecambe Bay wasn't exactly a major hub of the kelp-oil industry, but the professor was a Londoner, and didn't know any different. In his view, the key word in his judgment was presumably "retreated." Although he doubtless meant no insult to Lancaster's status as a center of learning, it still counted as provincial in his world-view, which regarded Oxford and Cambridge as suburbs of London in spite of the geographical evidence to the contrary, and everywhere beyond the geographical Oxford as "the north." On the other hand, he probably thought of all academic life as a quiet retreat from the hubbub of bioindustrial activity whose British heart, if not its soul, was Rosalind's empire. He knew that, as Rowland's best friend, I could have walked into Rosalind's employment the day after graduation, and at any time thereafter. He probably regarded my failure to do so as a chronic lack of self-confidence.

Perhaps he was right. Perhaps, in fact, he was understating the case, and it had really been rank cowardice in the face of someone who wasn't even an enemy, strictly speaking. In my view, of course, I was simply showing solidarity with Rowland, who might well have taken it as an insult if I had gone to work for Rosalind, even if I hadn't done it until after Magdalen had returned to England...perhaps especially if I had done so after Magdalen's return.

The professor must have felt that his lack of enthusiasm was impolite, given my heroic efforts to build up his own specialty, because he was quick to backtrack on his lukewarm judgment. "Important work, though, algal studies, quite apart from the marine oil industry" he said. "We don't really know, as yet, how badly the littoral ecosystems were hit by the ecocatastrophe, do we? They were in the front line, after all, forced into rapid geographical shifts during the Antarctic Depletion. The resettlement isn't simply going to put things back the way they were— it's going to be a century or more until we can even measure the lingering effects, and evolution would be in tachytelic mode even if human creativity weren't playing such a strong hand. How is the work going?"

"Slowly," I said, philosophically. After "still the same old stuff," there is no more hallowed response in the corridors of academe. One's research is always going slowly, and one always has to admit the fact with an expression of philosophical resignation. In my case, though, it was true, and not because of the ever-pressing demands of teaching. Had I been working for Rosalind, of course, everything would have been different. In the Hive of Industry, everything moved rapidly. Urgency was the norm, philosophical resignation was prohibited, and results flowed in abundance, nourishing the world as the infant Zeus had once been nourished by Amalthea's magical horn.

There was still some time to go before the ceremony was due to begin—the professor and I had been standing relatively close to the marquee when crowd dynamics began to move us, and we'd been among the first inside, although we'd naturally taken up positions in the rear, as befitted our lowly status. We had no alternative but to go on making conversation, and the Professor inevitably followed the script dictated by Fate.

"Do you know what it is that Rowland's doing, out in the Orinoco delta?" he asked. "I haven't seen any of his recent publications, I fear."

"Not exactly," I admitted. "He's not very good at keeping in touch—and he doesn't publish at all, so you haven't actually missed out on anything—but we're still friends." I felt compelled to add the last remark, simply because the fact seemed so vulnerable to doubt.

"I've seen images of his gargantuan mud hut on the web," the Professor said. "Quite an achievement in itself, though not as elegant as Roderick's Pyramid. You and Rowland both did elective courses in civil engineering, didn't you? Rowland was determined to match his grandfather's qualifications as a true Renaissance Man, wasn't he? You both did Practical Neurology too, as I remember, with old Fliegmann—he died five years ago, alas. You were keeping Rowland company, I assume—lending moral support. Magdalen stuck more narrowly to the central syllabus, as I recall. She was intelligent enough, but she didn't have Rowland's vaulting imagination." Dutifully—because he hadn't, after all been my personal tutor—he didn't add: "Nor had you."

"Rowland had a lot of interests," I confirmed. "I tried to keep up, but I couldn't. Magdalen, having grown up with him, had already given up, although Rosalind didn't approve. Rosalind had intended them to be equals and collaborators—and she was probably right to believe that Magdalen was Rowland's equal intellectually, only made timid by the backwash of his energy and his arrogance."

"Arrogance is no sin in a scientist," the professor observed—perhaps plaintively, since he was not an arrogant man himself. "The great ones always had infinite faith in themselves, and no respect at all for orthodoxy. That kind of attitude fuels the drive, the necessary obsession."

He wasn't just expressing regret for his own lack of that drive, and his own lack of greatness. He was looking at me. He had no right to do that. He didn't know me at all.

"I expect that Rowland will come down from the Pyramid with the other family members, when the ceremony's just about to start," the professor opined, when I didn't make any reply to his last remark. "I don't know his other sisters, but I'd certainly recognize Rosalind if I saw her—she wasn't mingling outside, was she?"

"Rosalind doesn't *mingle*," I said, flatly. "But I didn't see any of the sisters either. I met most of them, when Rowland and I were still students, but they were all kids back then—Rosalind left a long gap after the first two, presumably to give her time to see how the experiment was working out. The older ones will have grown up now, and even the little ones I met will be teenagers. It's ten years since I've seen any of them—they wouldn't remember me."

"I'm surprised by that...that you didn't keep in touch with the family," the professor ventured, probing as subtly as he could, because he knew that he was on sensitive ground.

"I shouldn't have let things slide," I admitted. "I wish that Magdalen had taken the trouble to call me, though, if...when..." I couldn't finish the sentence. If, or when Magdalen had decided to kill herself, she probably hadn't called anyone. I wasn't the only one she hadn't turned to *in extremis*.

"You were...quite fond of her, though, back then?"

"Yes," I confirmed, through teeth that were only slightly gritted, "quite fond."

He knew when a subject had to be dropped, and returned to safer ground. "I thought that Roland would make an insect man back then," he said, settling back into his rut, in terms of his phraseology as well as his subject-matter. "In spite of all the flirtations with strange sidelines, I thought he'd eventually take up where Roderick had left off, Rosalind having gone off at something of a tangent."

"According to the Usher family doctrine," I said, only a trifle sarcastically, "there's no such thing as an insect man *per se*. In Roderick the Great's vocabulary, insects are components of *dedicated symbiotic partnerships*; their early evolution took place in harness with the evolution of flowering plants, as a complex *pas de deux*. In Usher mythology, an insect's place is in the bosom of a flower, trading its services as a pollen-distributor for nectar."

"You're being flippant," he said. "That might apply, albeit loosely, to bees, but insects are extraordinarily versatile, ecologically speaking—almost as versatile as worms. Only a tiny minority are involved in pollination, or any other kind of symbiosis, and then only as imagoes."

"That was the past, Professor," I reminded him. "The Ushers are looking to the future. From now on...from fifty years ago, in fact...the fate of insects is to be whatever the Hive of Industry wants them to be. Pests out, symbiotes in, no neutrals. Anyway, insects were never all that versatile. There might still be hundreds of thousands of beetle species left, out of the pre-Crash millions, but they're all just beetles. The insects never contrived to recolonize the sea in the way that reptiles, mammals and birds did. There aren't any insects in my little corner of creation—yet."

"You're still being flippant," was Professor Crowthorne's expert judgment. Gallantly, he added: "And why not? We take ourselves and our work too seriously, sometimes—and in the face of tragedy, of matters that we can't control, no matter how clever we might be as biotechnicians, what psychological weapons do we have, except for a refusal not to take things too seriously? You have to laugh or you'd cry—isn't that what they say up there in Lancashire."

His idea of northern parlance had obviously been forged by historical dramas on TV, but he meant well.

"So it's rumored," I agreed.

CHAPTER THREE

Fortunately, the family members were beginning to make their appearance and fill up the front rows of the auditorium. The daughters didn't enter in a disciplined file, but there was an order of sorts to their gradual filtration. The older ones were looking after the younger ones. I wasn't really counting—I was looking for Rowland, still believing that he was bound to appear—but I couldn't help being aware that the daughters were more than a dozen strong, perhaps nearer to twenty in total.

Rowland didn't appear. Maybe, I thought, right up until the last possible moment, he was going to come in last, escorting Rosalind as a dutiful son should. Maybe, I thought, the tragedy of Magdalen's suicide—or Magdalen's death, if it had been accidental—had brought them together in grief, had healed their differences and united the family again. Maybe, I thought, there might be something resembling a happy ending to place in the credit column against the debit of Magdalen's loss, to provide some crumb of consolation, if not to produce some impossible semblance of balance in the books.

But Rowland didn't appear. When Rosalind finally made her grand entrance, she was alone: unaccompanied, unsupported, devoid of any symbiotic partnership, dedicated or otherwise.

How could I ever have thought that it might be otherwise? *Of course* Rosalind was alone. If Rowland had been there, he would have been sent to sit down, not allowed to stand beside Rosalind, or even slightly behind her.

She was perfectly composed, and quite beautiful, in her own

way. In an era of sophisticated somatic engineering, any woman can be beautiful, in a conventional sense, but distinctive beauty is still rare and precious, and Rosalind had it, more than any of her beautiful daughters. She wasn't as pretty as Magdalen, as charming as Magdalen or as lovable as Magdalen, but she was more beautiful, not because of her metallic blonde hair or her striking pale blue eyes, or the delicacy of her nose, or the symmetry of her ears and chin, but because she was Rosalind, the Queen Bee, in all her absolute majesty. Web chatter sometimes likened her to Cleopatra or Catherine the Great, but those models were morally compromised; the most frequently-cited analogy by far was to Elizabeth I, the Virgin Queen.

Rosalind had twenty children, but she had never married, and never would. The idea was unthinkable. Unlike Elizabeth, she didn't even have "favorites." She was always unescorted, at social occasions of every sort.

She looked magnificent. I had no doubt that she would be magnificent. It was Magdalen's funeral, but it was her show.

"He's not here, is he?" said Professor Crowthorne, in a whisper that had horror in it as well as amazement.

"No," I said, in a much more level tone. "He's not here. He hasn't come."

My first instinct was not so much to explore possible reasons for Rowland's absence, but to find excuses for him—excuses I hadn't been able to find, in the event, for myself.

Perhaps Rowland and Magdalen had enjoyed—or had at least believed that they enjoyed—such a close union of mind and spirit that Rowland felt that his presence in spirit made any physical presence at her funeral quite irrelevant. Perhaps they had been so close—and yet, paradoxically, so far apart—that Rowland had been overwhelmed by grief. Perhaps he was ill in bed, unable to travel. Perhaps....

Rosalind, I knew, would not have tolerated any excuses of those sorts. She was the kind of hard-line positivist who thought all talk of "spirit" nonsensical; the only kind of presence she recognized was physical presence. Grief she did believe in, but did not believe that it could or should be incapacitating. Illness she undoubtedly believed in too, but similarly believed that it could not and should not be incapacitating, unless literally mortal. In Rosalind's view, I had no doubt, Rowland should have been sitting meekly in the front row, with all his sisters—perhaps positioned arrogantly at their head, but nevertheless with them, in the junior ranks of the family.

In theory, I suppose I agreed with her standpoint—but I admit to being a slightly fuzzy thinker, and when it came to Rowland, and Magdalen too, I was prepared to think in terms of spirit, and incapacitating grief. There had always been something slightly uncanny about Rowland, and if there was one person in the world who might be capable of surviving death as a ghost, in the minds of people who had known her, it was Magdalen. But still, Rowland should have been there. Whatever excuse he had, he should have set it aside, for Magdalen's sake.

I could only speculate, of course, as to the effect the Magdalen's return to Eden, after little more than a year in Venezuela—her desertion, as he would have seen it—must have had on Rowland. That was one of the many things about which he maintained absolute web-silence. I could understand that he might have felt deeply offended—angry, even—but not to the extent that he would refuse to attend her funeral.

Obviously, I wasn't the only person who had expected to see Rowland there, although there was probably only one other who had turned up for that express purpose, because there was a ripple of reaction when the other members of the crowd realized what the professor and I had realized. It wasn't exactly a murmur of disapproval, but it was audible and tangible. Magdalen's brother wasn't there: only her sisters, and her mother.

All eyes were on Rosalind anyway, but the general awareness of Rowland's absence focused that attention even more intently, and lent an extra dimension of sympathy to it.

Rosalind probably wasn't quite as old as Professor Crowthorne, but she was certainly in her seventies, at least. She had made far more use of somatic engineering to modify her appearance than he had, but she had been equally wise in not attempting to preserve the visual illusion that she might be in her twenties. She was not interested in seeming venerable, but she was even less interested in seeming youthful. She wanted to appear mature in her distinctive beauty, not because maturity implied wisdom, but because it implied power—real power, not the ineffectual sham manifested by such historical lightweights as Elizabeth I. The cast of her features was not masculine, but it was not feminine either, unless one assumed—as some syco-phantic commentators had been willing and eager to do—that it was the type-specimen of a new femininity, which would even-tually redefine the notion.

She seemed capable of redefining such terms as "beautiful" and "regal," and I mean no insult in saying that the funeral brought out the best in her. She was clad in black, but she was no mute butterfly. She was a human Queen Bee from top to toe, in her sober and somber mourning-dress. Lesser mortals still hired minister-substitutes to act as masters-of-ceremonies in humanist funerals, but not Rosalind. Rosalind took the podium herself, and it was obvious that she would be in charge from beginning to end, no matter who else she might invite to eulo-gize or sing.

There were eulogies, of which Rosalind's was the most elegant, if not the longest; there was also music, some of it accompanied by voices. There was no mention, by anyone, of the cause of Magdalen's death. There was no mention either, by anyone, of Rowland. How Rosalind improvised a eulogy without mentioning that Magdalen had a twin of sorts, I'm not entirely sure, but she did. She spoke about her love for her first-born daughter, and her other daughters' love for their eldest sister, and she said something about Magdalen's significant contributions to the work of the Hive of Industry, but she never mentioned that Magdalen had ever visited Venezuela. I noticed those absences far more than the words that were actually pronounced, perhaps because I was numb with the shock of Rowland's absence.

As soon as the disbelief wore off, I resumed thinking, with

all the force that mentality could muster: *I shouldn't have come. I should have had the courage to stay away. If he could do it, why couldn't I?* I actually felt resentful. I felt as if I had somehow been tricked—as if the possibility of seeing Rowland had been dangled as a lure, but that, on taking the bait, I had found nothing but a cruelly-barbed steel hook.

It was nonsense, of course. I hadn't even been invited to the funeral, let alone lured. I had merely been given permission to attend, if I wished, not because I had once known Rowland, but because I had once known Magdalen. I had been given permission to attend because I had once loved Magdalen, very dearly, and because Rosalind had known that Magdalen—however she had died—would have wanted the people who had loved her dearly to be at her funeral. Rowland didn't come into it…except that what had sprung first and foremost to the minds of ingrates like myself and Professor J. V. Crowthorne, who had known and loved Magdalen as a component in a dedicated symbiotic relationship, had been the possibility of seeing the living remainder of that relationship, not the corpse of its extinct fraction.

Not that we actually got to see a corpse. There was a container, in the geometrical center of the circle mapped out by the dome's circumference, but it wasn't even a coffin. The legally-required cremation had already taken place, in private; all that was offered to the contemplation of the mourners was a casket the size of a tea-caddy, which presumably contained her ashes. I say *presumably* not because I doubted that she was really dead, or because I doubted that that the contents of the casket really were the residue of her cremation, or because I had any cynical reservations about identifying post-cremation ashes with a person, but simply because we had to presume. All we could actually see was a casket. We had to imagine its contents.

Would it have been better if we had been able to see her, rebeautified by the embalmer's art, lying on a silk cushion in a human-sized box? I doubt it—but the presence of the casket did serve to emphasize the mystery still surrounding her death. It did imply, however unreasonably, that there had been, and still was, something to hide.

In all probability, no one else in Britain would have been able to hide the circumstances of a death, in spite of all the legal and moral restrictions associated with the New Privacy, but the Ushers were true masters of the game of virtual invisibility. What they did not want to be known remained unknown; that was all there was to it.

The ceremony did not last long. It was over in ten minutes less than an hour, although a few minutes were left thereafter for silent contemplation. No one broke ranks while Rosalind was still standing there, head bowed. I thought for a moment or two that she was going to measure out the hour exactly, to the second, but she had too much style for that. The silence only lasted three minutes before the moment of suspension was officially ended, and Rosalind slipped into a new style of discourse to thank us all for coming.

She didn't apologize for the fact that no refreshments had been laid on, and that there was no be no "wake," but she did invite everyone to explore Eden at their leisure. She didn't say so, but the implication was that breathing the atmosphere of that sacred place was bound to reward the soul more lavishly than any supply of food and alcohol. As for filling the stomach—well, that was a vulgar business best left to the hidden recesses of the New Privacy.

The family then began to filter out as they had filtered in—except for Rosalind, who marched along the aisle to the main entrance, and stationed herself on the threshold in order to shake the hand of everyone in the audience, and thank them for coming.

That took a long time. Because Professor Crowthorne and I were a lot closer to the back than the front, we could have made a dash for it and got out into the open, sweet-scented air in less than five minutes, but neither of us was in a mood for dashing, and neither of us was in a hurry to look into Rosalind's eyes. A full fifteen minutes of awkward silence had elapsed before we were impelled forward by the ebb tide of the multitude and found ourselves on the threshold.

I let the professor go first.

"Professor Crowthorne," said Rosalind, who might have needed a subtle earpiece to remind her who some of our fellow mourners were, but gave every indication of recognizing Magdalen's former tutor at first glance. "Thank you for coming. Magdalen always spoke very highly of your enthusiasm as an educator, and the support you gave her when she first left home."

Apart from the "always," I figured that it might almost have been true. The professor did have enthusiasm as an educator; he might be a poor communicator in other respects, but when it came to waxing lyrical about his subject, he was a human dynamo. It went with the territory; I was in a position to understand that now. He would also have done his utmost to lend Magdalen moral support when she found herself in a strange institution, far from home—even though she already had the support of her loving brother.

"Peter," said Rosalind, moving on before I was quite ready. She seized the hand that I held out reflexively, but instead of the curt and tokenistic pressure she'd afforded to the professor, she actually hung on to mine. "Thank you for coming. I need to talk to you. I'm busy just now, as you can see, but if you wouldn't mind waiting—please take a look around the Palaces for an hour or two, and go up to the Pyramid whenever you please. I'll try to be there by four o'clock, but I'm sure you'll understand if I'm a little late."

I opened my mouth as if to reply, but she had released my hand as soon as she reached the end of her sentence, and I knew that she neither wanted nor expected a reply—not even the merest sign of assent. The Queen had spoken; I, her subject, had only to obey. Still in the grip of the current that was flowing onwards and outwards, I found myself outside, in the soft spring sunlight, amid the sweet scents and the black butterflies. Was it only an illusion that the latter now seemed more abundant?

Helplessly, I checked my watch. It was ten past one; the ceremony had begun at noon. Rosalind expected me to kick my heels for the best part of three hours—and then to forgive her if she was "a little late."

"Well," said Professor Crowthorne, "*that*'s quite a privilege."

"Is it?" replied, automatically. My voice was a trifle hoarse, so the acid sarcasm didn't quite come out as intended.

"What do you suppose she wants?" the professor asked, curiously.

What do you think she wants, you silly old fool? I didn't reply. Aloud, and meekly, all I said was: "I expect she wants to ask me about Rowland. She probably imagines that we're still in touch. She wants to ask me why he's not here—she probably thinks he told me that he wasn't going to come, and left it to me to explain why."

"I was surprised when he didn't come in with the rest of the family," the professor observed, although he'd already expressed his surprise more eloquently than any mere report could contrive. Reaching for even deeper levels of banality, he added: "A pity, that—I was hoping to see him. Surely he must have warned his mother that he wasn't going to be here, though?"

I shouldn't have come, I thought. "Actually," I said, "Rowland being Rowland, I'd have been surprised if he *had* given Rosalind prior notice of his absence. But I'm genuinely surprised that he isn't here. I expected him to be here. I suppose I'm not surprised that he didn't warn me either—but I wish he had."

"Rather bad form, in my opinion," Professor Crowthorne continued. "I mean, there's nothing unusual about boys falling out with their mothers, especially when their mothers are as… forceful…as Ms. Usher—but missing your own sister's funeral! And the closest sister of them all! I know they weren't really twins, in the sense that they shared a womb, but they were the same age."

Rowland and Magdalen had been incubated ectogenetically, and they were the produce of different sperm-donors, but they had, indeed, been born within a few hours of one another, having always been envisaged as a pair: a dedicated symbiotic unit.

"How old are you and Rowland now?" the professor went on, when I didn't step in to fill his pause. "Thirty-six? Thirty-seven? Too old to be nursing adolescent grudges, that's for sure. This could have been a golden opportunity to build bridges, mend fences, heal wounds. Rowland should have been here, for his own sake as well as his mother's."

And mine, I thought. "It's not that easy," I said, weakly. "We're in a brave new world now. The old clichés don't apply any more."

"Are you quoting Shakespeare or Huxley?" he asked, although the obvious answer was both. "Either way, you're wrong. The whole point of the Usher family's endeavors has been to save and preserve the civilization we took thousands of years to build, and they succeeded. They weren't alone, of course, but there was no one more committed than they were to the cause. The old norms still apply—and so they should, since we had to fight so hard to preserve them. Rowland should have been here."

Obviously, I wasn't the only one who felt resentful that my hopes and expectations had been dashed. I'd moved on from there, though. The fact that my hopes of seeing Rowland had been relegated to the dead past was now a mere matter of circumstance. What was occupying my mind at present was the fact that Rosalind wanted to see me. She had fixed a rendez-vous for four o'clock, at the Pyramid—although she naturally reserved the right to be late, if more pressing matters of duty intervened.

She undoubtedly wanted to ask me about Rowland—and I didn't have anything to tell her. If there was one prospect in the world more terrifying than being summoned into the imperial presence to bear witness, it was that of being summoned into the presence knowing in advance that I was not in a position to satisfy her desire. I had nothing to tell her, and I knew that telling her nothing, however honest and accurate it might be, was not going to satisfy her.

"I wish I could keep you company," Professor Crowthorne

said, perhaps sincerely. "I'd quite like to take a look around the Palaces, and I'm sure that you could give me the next best thing to a family-guided tour, but I'm at the mercy of the train time-table, and I have to get back to the Great Wen tonight. I'll have to walk to the station—there's no prospect of a taxi, given the size of the crowd."

I wondered whether he knew where the custom of refer-ring to London as "the Great Wen" had originated, but I wasn't about to ask him, or attempt any kind of discussion about the Romantic response to the Industrial Revolution, and I certainly wasn't about to make any observation about Hell being a city much like London. He was right about the impossibility of getting a cab, though. There was already a considerable outflow through the gate, and the vehicles lying in wait had already been commandeered. We were in rural Devon, after all—the local taxi, while not exactly an endangered species, was something of a *rara avis*. At least half of the invitees were evidently familiar with Eden, and had no need to take advantage of Rosalind's invitation to look around, so there was something of a mass exodus in progress..

"That's all right," I said. "I'll walk with you, if you like—I'll have plenty of time to get back here again before four, even if your train's late."

I meant no more than I said, but my mind was still a little numb. Was I secretly harboring an intention to hop on the London train with him, in order to pick up a northbound connection from Bristol before nightfall?—so secretly that I dared not even confess it to myself. Perhaps. After all, I had the same excuse as he did. By the time I had seen Rosalind at four, it wouldn't be possible for me to get all the way back to Lancaster by train; I'd have to stay overnight, in Bristol or Birmingham if not in Exeter. I too was at the mercy of the timetable—but there had been no possibility of saying that to Rosalind's face while I was in a handshaking queue, so the only possibility I had of acting on temptation was to slip away quietly, and simply not turn up to the abruptly-scheduled meeting. Rosalind could hardly deem that a terrible sin, given that her own son had failed to turn up to his twin sister's funeral, of which he must have been given adequate notice.

The professor was obviously not averse to the idea having company on the walk, we set off together—but as we approached the gate, I saw the security men exchange glances. They were inside the gates, now, bidding polite farewells to the exiting crowd. In imitation of their employer, they did indeed bid Professor Crowthorne a polite farewell, and thanked him warmly for coming. To me, however, the man in charge said: "Rosalind would prefer it if you would remain in the grounds, Mr. Bell."

Even her Praetorian Guard referred to her by her given name, and not as "Ms. Usher."

That was all that was said—there was no vestige of a threat. I could not imagine that any of the burly men would physically retrain me if I insisted on leaving, even if I didn't tell them that I intended to come straight back after seeing the professor off. The simple fact was, however, that "Rosalind would prefer it if I would remain in the grounds," and they could not imagine that anyone in the world would not want to comply with Rosalind's preferences, today of all days.

The professor certainly couldn't imagine it. "It's perfectly all right, Peter," he assured me. "I really don't mind walking on my own. It was good to see you again. We really must make more effort to keep in touch. Occasions like this serve as a salutary reminder of the need to maintain contacts, don't you think?"

"Yes," I said, "they certainly do."

I let him walk away, while I turned back, a prisoner of my error. I shouldn't have come—but I had, and now I was trapped. Now I had to face up to Rosalind, unarmed.

CHAPTER FOUR

Having little or no alternative, I did as Rosalind had suggested, and took a stroll around Eden—or, more specifically, its Crystal Palaces. I was by no means the only person taking advantage of Rosalind's regal invitation, but I no longer felt part of a crowd going with a general flow. None of the other strollers in the great glass houses was waiting for an interview with Rosalind; in that respect, I was alone, and that was exactly how I felt. I was no longer *in the company* of those who had merely been given the freedom of the grounds and were taking advantage of the fact. I was moving through a parallel reality, in a different direction.

Relatively few of my fellow mourners were prisoners of the railway timetable, of course. Only the rich have private cars nowadays, but there weren't very many people who could count themselves intimates of Magdalen and Rosalind who weren't either rich or employees, and none of the employees had far to go if and when they left the grounds. Those who were prisoners of the timetable had grabbed all the available taxis, or settled for walking to the station, but there were plenty of people in no hurry, who welcomed the opportunity to take a peek at the latest wonders of the Hive of Industry. Under different circumstances, I might have thought the opportunity welcome myself, but as things were, I experienced my freedom to roam as a mere mockery, an ironic inversion of my captivity.

There was a sense, of course, in which Rosalind's Crystal Palaces were merely glorified greenhouses, some of them laid out as showcases of past achievements, others dedicated to the careful cultivation of plants that weren't yet ready, or licensed, for outdoor cultivation. The time was long gone when plants needed much protection from the British weather, which had been well-disciplined by the ingenious wind farms that surrounded the shores of the various islands in the group, reducing transatlantic hurricane-relics to light breezes that the Met Office could virtually steer at will, but experimentation demanded conditions controlled to a much finer degree than practical meteorologists could contrive, and many of the Hive's products were, in any case, designed for hotter climes than ours. At least half the palaces were tropical.

The tropical houses were the most popular with certain elements of the remaining crowd, but I was working up enough of a sweat without assistance, so I stuck to the temperate ones. I wasn't running any risk of being dosed with insidious psychotropics: the flowers producing active scents were all being grown under bell-jars, with networks of rubber tubing to siphon off the product for concentration and testing. The plants that didn't have that double layer of insulation were guaranteed harmless, and the fact that each and every species was accompanied in the grounds of its own palace by its specialist pollinator didn't create any risk of being stung. The first thing that Roderick the Great had done in producing new bee species by the score had been to take away their weaponry. His collaborators had not been able to do the same with the wasp species they had engineered as specialist predators, but wasps were becoming rare now, at least in England, having done their designated jobs so efficiently as to reduce the pest populations they were attacking to minimum reproductive level.

"Minimum reproductive level" was another of Roderick's catch-phrases. "Extinction" was not merely a dirty word nowadays but a dirty concept; he had never seen it as part of his mission to drive any organism to extinction—merely to render those that were inconvenient to human need and human comfort rare and unobtrusive. The effects of the ecocatastrophe had, of course, resulted in a dramatic loss of biodiversity in every stratum of the ecosphere, but Roderick had wanted to keep his hands clean in that respect, and he could legitimately claim that the increase in biodiversity prompted by the application of his methods had offered considerable compensation for Nature's slaughter.

All in all, though, the insects had come through the holocaust reasonably well. Even species whose extinction would not have raised a single tear had pulled through. Bedbugs and various species of human louse still survived—but not in the beds or on the heads of honest citizens of the British Republic...or, for that matter, dishonest ones.

I was able to take an interest in the plants, of course; I would have been able to do that even if they had simply been pretty and nicely-perfumed, but I still had some expertise in flower design left over from my days at university, so I was better able than any mere gawker to appreciate the effort that was on display in Rosalind's showcases and experimental plots. From the view-point of her current thinking, *everything* on public display was presumably old hat to a greater or lesser degree, but innovation moved so rapidly in the Hive of Industry that even material that Rosalind had recently cast aside as *passé* still seemed state-of-the-art to a specialist in marine algae.

I was impressed by the sexiness of the flowers, and not because the bell-jars containing those engineered to produce synthetic pheromones were leaking. The sexiness of flowers had long been one of Rosalind's preoccupations, and she had not been immune to educative zeal herself in the days when I had visited Eden with Rowland. She it was, in person, who had lectured me on the historical ramifications of the strange controversy that the great Linnaeus had caused by electing, on rational grounds, to make the reproductive organs of plants the basis for his classification—a decision that some censorious individuals had condemned as obscene. Of course, she had dutifully pointed out, the cause of immodest rationality had not been helped by the fact that writers like Thomas Stretser had immediately co-opted the vocabulary of Linnaean botany for use as a euphemistic code for description of the functioning of the human genitalia, in such classics of perverse pornography as *The Natural History of the Frutex Vulvaria; or, Flowering Shrub* and *Arbor Vitae; or, The Natural History of the Tree of Life,* both by-lined Philogynes Clitorides. Rosalind owned illustrated editions of both texts, as well as first editions of Erasmus Darwin's *The Botanic Garden*, including his poetic account of "The Loves of the Plants," and Sir William Jones's translation of the floral-erotic Indian epic *Sacontalá*. She was also the proud owner of several paintings by Georgia O'Keeffe.

As an honored visitor to Eden, I had been required to study all those specimens of peculiar eroticism, not only in Rosalind's company but in Magadalen's—and, of course, Rowland's. It had not been an entirely comfortable series of experiences.

"Flowers evolved in order to be beautiful," Rosalind had once told me, "and not merely to be beautiful, but to be sensual. Don't ever make the mistake of thinking that because natural selection designed them to appeal to the aesthetic sensibilities of insects, any appeal they make to human aesthetics is mere coincidence. Beauty *is* in the eye of the beholder, not to mention the organs of touch, hearing, taste and smell, but in terms of what our sense organs report to us, and how that information is neurologically translated into sensation and experience, all complex organisms have a great deal more in common than was once imagined. You're a geneticist, so you're well enough aware of the degree of kinship that exists between all organisms."

"Some insects are beautiful too," I remembered pointing out, "but some very definitely aren't."

"And some are both," Rowland had chipped in. "Butterflies, dragonflies and the like all start off as ugly larvae."

"Which means," Rosalind had observed, "that beauty is attainable, even from ugly raw material, if only you have the trick of it. That what the real mission of genetic engineering is: to produce beauty...including, and perhaps especially, the beauty that is the true soul of erotic attraction, and stands in desperate need of purification."

Given that kind of mind-set on the part of the genius of the place, it's hardly surprising that the Crystal Palaces of Eden were filled with flowers that were truly beautiful, not merely in terms of their color, design and scent but in terms of the way they felt to the touch: their softness and their delicacy. It wasn't the case that every bed of flowers was an orgy of sorts, but it was impossible not to take the suggestion that they might be: that botanical debauchery was not only possible, but potentially capable of surpassing any other kind. There were flowers whose petals were colored in such a way as to resemble childlike faces, and flowers designed to recall other parts of the human anatomy. Natural selection had, of course, got there long before Rosalind, in the artistry of orchids, but natural selection had always been an amateur, and had always been slow in its endeavors. Rosalind was a professional, and lightning fast by comparison.

Not only did the time pass quickly as I wandered, lonely as a cloud, through hosts of every kind of flower under the sun, but I actually began to enjoy myself, once I had settled my mind to absorption in my surroundings and shoved anxiety aside, *pro tempore*.

What, after all, did I have to worry about? Rosalind would ask me about Rowland; I would explain, apologetically, that I hadn't heard from him; end of story. She wouldn't want to spin things out any longer than I did, today of all days. All she wanted was to ask a question, and it wasn't my fault that I didn't have the ghost of an answer. I wouldn't even mention the inconvenience that she'd caused me; I'd simply take the next available train to Bristol, and stay overnight there while awaiting the first northbound train in the morning. It was no big deal.

There is something essentially restful about the beauty of temperate flowers, and the quiet hum of friendly insects. Perhaps there was also a little something in the air of the Palaces, in spite of the bell-jars—something tranquilizing, if not actually euphoric.

It was not until five to four that I presented myself at the main door of the pyramid, and explained to the concierge that I had an appointment with Rosalind. I suspect that he was well aware of it, and only made a show of checking his palm to remind me who was boss, but he let me in, and had a junior employee guide me to the appropriate reception-room.

The pyramid was a very large structure; although its footprint was only a little larger than that of the Great Pyramid of Cheops, it was a good deal taller, its four faces being much more steeply sloped. The elevator buttons were numbered all the way up to thirty-two, but I knew that there were at least four floors above that, accessible only by strictly private means.

I was taken up to thirty, which seemed a little high for my obvious unimportance in the scheme of the Hive's dealings, although I had been up considerably higher in the past. The room into which I was shown had a spectacular view, not merely of Eden but a substantial fraction of Exmoor, but I didn't go to the window to stare out. I don't usually suffer unduly from acrophobia, but I felt that the last thing I needed at present was any hint of vertigo. Instead, I sat down and waited.

Punctuality, they say, is the politeness of princes—which primitive generalization embraces queens—but Rosalind wasn't being insulting in turning up twenty minutes late. She really was having a very busy day, and she had a lot on her mind.

She offered me a drink. I asked for a glass of water. She poured it for me, along with something a little stronger for herself.

"Thank you for coming, Peter," she said, by way of an opening. "Magdalen would have wanted you to be here." Then she added: "I assume that Rowland didn't tell you he wouldn't be coming, any more than he told us?" That wrong-footed me completely, shattering all my expectations at a stroke.

"I haven't heard from him recently," I said, glad to be able to offer it as a confirmation rather than an unwelcome reply to a probing inquiry."

Rosalind sat down beside me. I tried to tell myself that she wasn't trying to be intimidating, that she found close proximity no other human beings as awkward as I did, but I knew how disciplined she was, and how determined. She looked directly into my eyes. I couldn't sustain her gaze for more than a second, now, even though I had trained myself, ten years before, to meet even her gaze, if and when the occasion warranted it, for as long as a minute.

Think of her as a work of art, I had told myself, then. *Think of her as an artifice of exquisite beauty, not as a conscious human being. And if all else fails, remember that she's a scientist, with a mind trained to objectivity.*

There was no possibility of any psychological ploy of that sort working now. I tried to concentrate hard on my glass of water, looking down into its transparent depths.

She actually reached out and put her hand on my wrist, in a confidential and affectionate manner that was completely different from a formal and impersonal handshake. I had never known her do that before, even to Rowland or Magdalen.

"I'm worried about him, Peter," she said. "I need to ask you for a favor."

Oddly enough, that hit me like a bolt from the blue. In retrospect, perhaps I should have expected it. In retrospect, it almost seemed obvious—but it hadn't seemed obvious in advance. Queen Rosalind of the Hive of Industry was asking me for a favor. Even though there was no logical reason why she shouldn't, the idea had seemed somehow unthinkable.

"What favor?" I said, warily, and perhaps not altogether politely. In retrospect, I should have asked: "Why are you worried about him?"—but I didn't. I had to know what favor it was that she wanted from me.

She was still touching my arm. "I want you to go to Venezuela," she said. "I want you to visit Rowland—not for my sake, I hasten to add, but for his."

I was so stunned I had virtual concussion. "Venezuela?" I repeated feebly. "I can't...." That was entirely the wrong way to go about it, of course.

"Yes you can," said Rosalind, firmly. "Whatever obstacles are in your path can be cleared. If you need some sort of financial recompense, you only have to say the word—but I know that it's not something you'd do for money. It's something you'll do because you're Rowland's friend, and because he needs you. You do still think of yourself as his friend, don't you?"

What could I say to that? What could I have said, even if it hadn't been true?

"Yes," I said, "but...."

"But you don't feel that you can take my word for it that he needs you," she said, effortlessly usurping the nascent statement and turning it to her own advantage. She removed her gentle hand from my wrist. "You'd rather hear it from him, I suppose, but you won't...and that's the most important reason why he needs you. I'm not asking you to be my ambassador, to try to patch things up between us, and I'm certainly not asking you to be my spy, to report back to me on exactly what he's doing out there in that glorified termite-mound of his. I'm just asking you to be his friend, because I have reason to believe that he needs a friend just now. He needs someone to be with him, to talk to him, to provide some balance in his life, at least for a while. I don't know how long that will take—I leave you to judge for yourself. Just be reassured that, no matter how long it takes, you won't be the loser by it. If you're still as determined now as you were ten years ago not to enter my employ, that's fine—but know that the job you have is absolutely safe, and that if you want to move on, nothing will stand in the way of your ending up exactly where you want and need to be—put please, please, do as I ask and go to Venezuela."

It wasn't the thought of going to South America that made me hesitate. I'd come all the way to Exeter and beyond in the hope of seeing Rowland, and a plane journey to Trinidad wasn't that much longer than a twice-interrupted train-journey across most of the length to England, although the subsequent boat-trip to the mouth of the Orinoco would doubtless add an extra day. I did want to see Rowland, and I was prepared to go to South

America to do it, even if I had to pay my own plane fare—and I certainly wasn't going to let Rosalind pay for it—but that wasn't the point. The point was, did Rowland want to see me? Even if he had no idea that Rosalind had asked me to do it, as a favor to her, would he want to see me? Would he answer the door, if I were rude enough and foolish enough to turn up unannounced? And if I managed to get a message through to him asking for permission, wouldn't he simply say no, even if he bothered to reply?

I should never have come, I thought. *And having come, I should simply have gone. That security guard wouldn't have—couldn't have—stopped me.*

But I had come, and I hadn't gone when I'd had half a chance. I had stayed, in answer to Rosalind's plea…and now, she was making another, much more demanding plea. I should have expected it—but I hadn't. I couldn't refuse, of course—that was unthinkable—but I could hesitate, at least for a few minutes. I could even prevaricate, in a tokenistic fashion.

"Why do you think he needs me?" I said, feebly—and even corrected that, hurriedly, to: "Why do you think he needs anybody?"

"Don't you think he needs someone, right now?" she countered. "After all, you're his friend. You know him as well as I do." A low blow, that last one. There was no polite reply to that.

"I don't know," I said, truthfully. "He's always been an independent character, and he's always been a trifle uncommunicative, so I don't like to read too much into his recent silence."

"But you were expecting to see him here today, weren't you?" she said, playing yet another trump card. "You must feel that his absence is so unusual as to be cause for alarm."

"I don't know why he wouldn't come," I had to admit.

"It was Magdalen's funeral," Rosalind said, emphatically, ramming home her irresistible advantage. "Can you imagine Rowland—the Rowland you knew, ten years ago—refusing to come to Magdalen's funeral?"

I couldn't answer that, so I lowered my head and took another sip of water. That was a mistake too. I should have said something to keep the exchange focused on Rowland.

"I'm sorry, Peter," she said, suddenly changing tack. "That was insensitive of me, wasn't it? You were in love with Magdalen once, weren't you?"

I kept my head down and said nothing. She didn't reach out to touch me again, though—she'd already fired that shot, and didn't see any need to repeat it.

"I'm sorry that didn't work out, in retrospect," she said. "It wasn't something I encouraged or discouraged, at the time...but if it had worked out, Rowland might not be in South America... and Magdalen might not be dead."

That was an even lower blow, and I couldn't help reacting. "What's that supposed to mean?" I asked, too sharply.

"Oh, my God!" she said, suddenly seeming confused—or putting on a convincing show. "I didn't mean to imply that you were in any way responsible...please, Peter, you can't suspect me of that. If anyone's to blame for this...for all of this...it's me. I can't deny that, and I'm not at all sure that I can make amends for it. I'm not even sure that you can help—but I do want you to try, if you're willing, because if anyone *can* help, it's you. The last thing I want is for Rowland to go the same way as Magdalen, if...."

She stopped there, ever the master tactician. She wasn't going to be the one to voice the suggestion that Rowland might already be dead, and that the only reason he hadn't come to Magdalen's funeral might be that he couldn't, or the corollary suspicion that, even if he were still alive at present, he might be in imminent danger of going "the same way as Magdalen."

I wasn't going to voice any suspicion of that kind either. "I'll call him," I said, knowing that I had to promise her something. "If he gives me permission to visit, I'll go to Venezuela—as soon as I can."

She wanted more than that. "I think you should insist," she said. "And if he doesn't answer, I really do think you need to go, in order to find out why. Not for my sake—I know you don't owe me anything—but for Rowland's. It's too late, alas, to do anything for Magdalen's sake, but if she were still alive, I think she'd be here instead of me, begging you to go."

Laying her lovely hand on my arm, I thought. *Looking me in the eyes, as brazenly as she could.* If Magdalen had still been alive, of course, I wouldn't have been there to be begged…but that was a mere quibble.

"I'll do what I can," I promised, knowing as I did it that I was promising too much—but knowing, too, that I had absolutely no alternative.

She might, after all, have been right. Rowland might need me, whether he could admit it or not. I had to go. Rosalind knew that. She had only commanded me do it because she knew that I couldn't command myself.

CHAPTER FIVE

I could have called Rowland from the train, but I didn't want to do that. Putting it off until I got back to Lancaster didn't make the homeward journey any easier, because I felt like an aristocrat in a tumbrel, on the way to the guillotine, every inch of the way, but it seemed more appropriate to call from home, from my own tiny republic, rather than from anyone else's turf.

Fortunately, I had a good reason for calling, a justification for opening communication.

He didn't answer his phone, of course—who does, nowadays?—and his answerphone wasn't equipped with the customary simulation of his face, fitted to an AI capable of holding an elementary conversation. All I got was a blank screen and a taped message inviting me to say my piece. There wasn't even a promise to get back to me. Rowland was no hypocrite.

"It's Peter," I said, although that datum would have been automatically recorded. "I've just got back from Magdalen's funeral. I expected to see you there. I hoped to see you there. The fact that I didn't see you there is worrying me intensely. We've been out of touch for far too long, and I'd really like to see you again. I'm more than willing to make the trip to Venezuela—I'm desperately in need of doing some tropical fieldwork, as it happens— but I'd be just as happy to see you here, if you're in the mood for a sight and taste of England. At any rate, I really would like some proof that you're still alive…and likely to remain so for the foreseeable future. Call me, please."

I literally watched the clock, knowing that if he didn't come back to me within five minutes, the ploy had probably failed—leaving me in something of a quandary. Four minutes elapsed before the bell chimed. I answered the phone myself—thus I suppose, answering my own question as to who ever bothered, in this day and age. *Anxious people* is the answer.

Images on phone screens aren't always reliable, but I didn't think that Rowland was the kind of person to employ electronic cosmetics. I assumed that I was looking at a live camera-feed, seeing him as he was. All things considered, he didn't look too bad. He'd always been handsome. In fact, the family resemblance between him and Rosalind was quite striking; the features looked almost as good on a man as on a woman, although no one would have thought of describing Rowland as "beautiful." Magadalen, perhaps fortunately in some ways, had favored her anonymous father.

"Peter," Rowland said, warmly. "I'm sorry it's been so long. I'm glad you went to the funeral. Magdalen would have wanted you to be there."

"She'd have wanted you to be there too," I couldn't help saying.

"I know," he said, with a sigh that sounded perfectly sincere. "It's just that it's so very difficult to leave my work. It's reached a very delicate stage. It's not the sort of operation that can be put on hold for days on end. Magdalen would have understood, I think—in fact, I'm sure of it. I wish with all my heart that she'd stayed here, you know. I knew that it wouldn't do her any good to go back to the Hive. That's what really killed her, you know, in spite of what Rosalind might have told you. You did see Rosalind, I assume?"

"Briefly," I admitted.

"And did she tell you that it was all my fault?"

"No," I said. "She even apologized, profusely, for accidentally hinting that it might have been mine."

"Yours?" Rowland seemed genuinely astonished. "How could it possibly have been yours? You haven't seen her in...it must be at least ten years."

I wondered how he knew that I hadn't. He must, I supposed, have maintained some sort of sporadic contact with Magdalen, even if he hadn't kept in touch with anyone else. Had that made things better or worse for her? Given that she was dead, it obviously hadn't done her much good.

"That was probably the point that Rosalind was making, if it wasn't really an accident," I said, mildly. "She might have been suggesting that if I'd maintained my relationship with Magdalen, on a *just friends* sort of basis, Magdalen might have been a little happier…and that maybe *a little* would have been enough to tip the balance. As I said, she took it back immediately, acknowledging the fact that it wasn't my failure, without seeking to lay the blame elsewhere."

"Typical," said Rowland. "She never did understand."

That was probably a trifle harsh. Rosalind had never been short of understanding; what she lacked was the empathy to calculate the consequences of her understanding. She was probably the world's foremost expert in olfactory psychotropics, but her knowledge of the art was purely scientific. I had no doubt at all that she had tried to "cure" the malaise of Magdalen's heart by that means, and had probably attributed her failure to incorrect dosage, or insufficient progress in chemical refinement. I could almost imagine her urging Magdalen to wake up and smell the roses, then watching and wondering as Magdalen's metaphorical stigmata continued to bleed from the thrust of imaginary thorns.

Rowland's thinking might or might not have been running along similar lines. At any rate, he changed the subject, very abruptly. "What sort of tropical fieldwork are you planning to do?" he asked. "You haven't gone into the oil business, I hope?"

I had, of course, included the remark about needing to do some tropical fieldwork merely to leave no stone unturned in my plea for an invitation to the Orinoco delta, but my ability to improvise was equal to the challenge.

"Coastlines went in and out everywhere in the course of the last century," I said. "New salt marshes sprang up by the thousand. I've been tracking natural genetic shifts in a number of different algal species, and I've found some interesting and peculiar phenomena—as you'd expect, given that algal cells are inherently simpler and more easily mutable than those of terrestrial plants. All the world's a cauldron, but the only place the soup really came to the boil is in the tropics. I need to figure out what kinds of change were precipitated in places where the pot was seriously stirred—where the rise in sea-level, limited as it was, disrupted vast areas and complex ecosystems. The river deltas in Africa and the Indian subcontinent suffered too much damage; I need to study an area that proved more resilient: the Amazon delta or the Orinoco delta. Of the two, the latter looks more promising—and you've gantzed a refuge smack in the middle of it. If you can supply me with a base for a few months, it might bring my work forward by an order of magnitude, and could well reveal some genuinely interesting genetic adaptation mechanisms."

What true scientist could possibly refuse a request couched in those terms? He was, after all, my friend.

Still, he hesitated.

"I'm not really equipped to receive visitors," he told me. "This isn't a research station, as such. I have a couple of people to help around the house, but no lab assistants, as such. I couldn't offer you anything remotely resembling adequate facilities for your kind of research."

"I can improvise," I assured him. "Even if there were an available alternative—which there isn't—I wouldn't want to take it, if there were a possibility of staying with you. We're friends, Rowland...aren't we?"

"Yes, of course," he said, automatically. "We'll always be friends...and we're fellow engineers, too, fighting the good fight against Nature's backlash, shoulder to shoulder. We don't have to be members of a Hive to pull together, to help one another out. If you need to be here, then of course you must come, but...."

I knew there'd be a *but*. I waited for him to spell it out. When he saw that I wasn't going to prompt him, he did—after a fashion.

"Look, Peter," he said, "I'm involved in some very difficult and delicate work here. I'd always intended to show it to you and explain it to you, when it had reached an appropriate stage of maturity. I'd always intended to invite you here, eventually, because I knew that you were the one person in the world guaranteed to understand it—but it hasn't reached that stage yet. On the other hand...."

He paused again. I wasn't sure why, this time. Something about his voice made me stare harder at the image on the screen, looking for signs of electronic enhancement. I was no longer sure that I was looking through the kind of camera that isn't supposed to lie.

"What's wrong?" he asked. My image was being transmitted directly. He had seen my expression change and my attention become more focused.

"Are you ill, Rowland?"

Enhanced or not, the image took on an expression that seemed slightly guilty. "No," he said, unconvincingly. "I'm perfectly okay, health-wise. I have been working very hard, though. I get a little tired, sometimes."

"Have you had a check-up recently?" I persisted. "I know that you're hundreds of miles from the nearest doctor, but you must have monitors and scanners there that can feed information to any med center in the world."

"I have all the equipment I could possibly need," he assured me. "The only reason I haven't had a check-up is that I don't need one. Did Rosalind tell you to ask these questions?"

"No," I replied. "She is worried about you, though. Maybe she can't believe that you wouldn't come to the funeral unless you were too ill to travel. You didn't even tell her that you weren't coming, did you?—let alone why."

"I'm busy," he repeated. "I'm not doing the kind of experiments that are over in a matter of hours or days. There are processes in hand, which set their own timetable. As I said, I always intended to let you in on it when it's ready, but it's not there yet…and it won't be finished in a matter of months, or even years. If you come here now, I'll help you fit out your own facilities to the best of my ability…but you might have to be patient with regard to an explanation of my work."

"That's not an issue," I assured him. "I do need reassurance that you're okay, though. I'll have work of my own to do, and you can take all the time you like explaining what you've been doing these last ten years, and why you haven't published anything."

"It's not finished," he repeated. "Not even the first phase."

"You haven't reached the end of the beginning," I said, trying to lighten the mood a little, "let alone the beginning of the end."

He smiled wryly. "I'd almost forgotten how glib you can be," he said. "Maybe I do need a little of that, as well as some meaty discussion. We used to have a good time, once, playing with words and ideas. I should have kept in touch…but it's never quite the same over the phone is it?"

"That's why we need to get together," I said. "Am I invited, then?"

"Of course," he said. "I'm just trying to warn you…But I suppose I do have facilities adequate for collecting and cataloguing the local algae. I have three boats, and if they don't suit your requirements, I can get one that is. I can make lab room for you easily enough, and if you want to bring an assistant, that's fine…provided that he or she is capable of discretion. I can't have information being leaked, Peter. I know that I can trust you—but I need to make that clear. I have to maintain secrecy, until I've perfected my procedures. You do understand, don't you?"

I didn't, yet—how could I, when he hadn't explained anything? What he was saying did help, slightly, to explain why he hadn't published anything in years, but only in a superficial sense. Science isn't supposed to have secrets. It's an innately collaborative endeavor, whose purpose is to bring knowledge into the light, to add to the sum of human understanding. The legendary wizards of old hoarded the wisdom they were supposed to have, deliberately hiding it away in order to maintain a monopoly—or, more likely, to conceal its idiocy and impotence—but real science is intrinsically opposed to that philosophy. Even in matters where money is at stake, because some discoverer or inventor wants to profit from his endeavor—and who doesn't?—there's an elaborate system of patents to protect financial interests while permitting and facilitating publication. That has been true for centuries, and in a time of ecological crisis, the pressure on scientists to reveal anything and everything that might be relevant to combating the crisis is more than a duty; it's a necessity. Rowland and I were living in interesting times; the survival of the species had been at risk for at least four generations, and would still be at risk for at least another four. Anyone who discovered anything that might help was morally obliged to make it known.

For the moment, however, all I could say was: "Okay. Whatever conditions you impose, I'll abide by them."

"Good," he said. "In that case, it will be very pleasant to see you again. You have no idea how starved I am of real conversation. *This* isn't the same." He waved his arm to indicate the telephonic apparatus that was connecting us. He was right about conversation not being the same over the phone, even if the cameras weren't rigged to lie. Electronic communication gives us sight and sound, but not presence. Real presence involves touch, and all kinds of olfactory stimuli of which we're not even consciously aware. A person can sit in front of a screen all day, talking to a hundred other people in turn, and still be "starved of real conversation," for lack of the authentic nourishment of presence.

Rowland had to be lonely. He had to be grateful for the fact that I wanted to visit, even if he hadn't been able to admit it to himself before, because of his passion for maintaining the secrecy of whatever it was that he was so determined to keep secret. In all likelihood, he really did need to see a friendly face, and to keep company with a friend for a while. I really would be doing him a favor.

"I'll call again as soon as I've got a timetable worked out," I said. "There are some formalities to clear up with the university, but there won't be any hitches. I hope to be on my way by the end of the week, if that's not too soon."

"No problem," he said. "Just let me know what you need, and I'll make what advance provision I can. We can sort out the details when you're here. There are inevitable delays in delivery way out here, but money talks, and I have plenty of that, thanks to dear old Roderick. I don't say that the impossible gets done at once when I snap my fingers, and even the possible takes time, but whatever we need, I can get."

I appreciated the *we*.

"That's great," I said—and bade him a temporary farewell, in order to set the wheels in motion.

That proved a good deal easier than might have been expected. I had to apply for instantaneous sabbatical leave, and provide immediate cover for all my teaching obligations. Given that one normally has to apply for sabbatical leave a year in advance, the dean of the faculty could have protested, but he didn't raise a murmur. I suspected, but didn't dare ask, that he'd already been contacted by the Hive, which had let him know that Rosalind would be greatly obliged if no obstacles appeared in my path, and that anything necessary to clear potential obstacles would be made available on request.

There is no one in the world more tractable than a university dean who has just been assured that any and all expenses will be met without question.

Since Rowland had raised the possibility spontaneously, I hesitated briefly over the matter of taking a lab assistant with me. Given that I really did intend to do some significant research while I was in a uniquely useful environment, an extra pair of hands would have been very useful, and I would undoubtedly have had my pick of the departmental research students had I cared to exploit that resource. No aspiring doctoral candidate would turn down the chance of a field trip to Rowland Usher's Orinoco redoubt, even if it delayed their thesis submission; as an item on a CV, it would be job-application gold. Indeed, even after I had decided to go alone, as soon as the news of my imminent departure for Venezuela got around, explicit requests were made that were practically pleas, and I felt bad about turning them down—and not because at least one of them had an implicit offer of sexual favors thrown into the attempted bargain as a makeweight.

I had to keep reminding myself that my primary purpose in making the trip was to make sure that Rowland was safe and sane, and that he would long remain so. I owed it to him not to clutter up the mission with too many potential distractions. Besides which, Rosalind might not have approved.

Inevitably, once I'd called Rowland to give him the provisional details of my itinerary, and had started packing for my departure, Rosalind called.

"Thank you, Peter," she said. "I really appreciate what you're doing."

I could have told her that I was doing it for Rowland, not for her, but it would have been dreadfully impolite, and perhaps not entirely honest. In reality, I was doing it for myself. What I said instead was: "I'm not going to be able to furnish you with full and regular reports from the Orinoco delta. If Rowland doesn't want me to call, I won't."

"I know that," she said. "I trust you to do everything possible to make sure that he's all right."

"You knew perfectly well that he was alive, when you talked to me in Eden, didn't you?" I said, to make sure that she didn't get off too lightly. "You must have some kind of spy-eye in the vicinity of his redoubt, if not actually inside."

"I knew that he was alive," she confirmed. "I'm sorry if I accidentally implied that there was a possibility that he wasn't."

"You wouldn't happen to know what the secret is that he's so determined to keep under wraps until he's ready to whip the curtain away, would you?"

"No, I don't," she said. "Nor am I expecting you to tell me what it is, once he's confided it to you. I just want to know that he's safe and sane—and I'm convinced that a few weeks and months in your company will increase the probability of his remaining safe and sane considerably."

I figured that I had built up a considerable balance of moral credit by now, and that Rosalind was as well-disposed to me at that moment as she'd ever been, or ever would be, so I screwed up my courage and asked *the* question.

"Why did Magdalen kill herself?" I asked, coming straight out with it because there as no way of approaching it subtly—although I didn't lose a second in adding; "I need to know, if I'm to talk to Rowland about it—and you do want me to talk to Rowland about it, don't you?"

For just a moment, Rosalind let her mask slip. She was on camera; she wasn't filtering her image. Even though she must have been expecting the question, at some stage, she wasn't quite ready for it at that moment. Perhaps she never would be.

"What makes you think she killed herself?" she hedged. I'd never seen her hedge before; it made her seem almost human.

"If she hadn't," I said, "you would have identified the cause of death at the funeral. Some secrets can't be kept, because the mere fact of trying to keep them is revelation enough."

"You're wrong about that," she snapped back. "Uncertainty is uncertainty, no matter how confident people are in their guesses. But you're right that you'll have to talk to Rowland about it, so I'll confirm your guess, and trust to your sense of honor not to let what I tell you go any further. You can tell him that Magdalen was poisoned, in circumstances which make it highly unlikely that the poisoning was accidental, and that she certainly wasn't murdered. As to why it happened…well, she didn't leave an explanatory note, and she didn't reveal very much in the conversations we had. I won't say that your guess is as good as mine, because it couldn't be, but any conjecture I offered regarding the exact causes of Magdalen's death, except in terms of immediate physical causation, would be just that: a guess."

That struck me as most un-Rosalind-like speech. It was almost as if she were deliberately beating around the bush, emphasizing what she didn't know in order to avoid specifying what she did know."

"Were you treating her?" I asked. "With psychotropics, I mean?"

"That's not relevant," she told me. "If I were, it would be entirely legal—I'm a licensed practitioner."

I hadn't been in the least concerned about matters of legality, and she knew it. She was deliberately misunderstanding me. Magdalen's death was obviously a very sore topic. Had I been in her presence, I would have apologized profusely for overstepping the mark, but over the phone, I felt that I had more license to ask questions.

She obviously thought so too. "This isn't a suitable topic for discussion over the phone," she said, flatly. "It might be useful for us to meet again before you leave, though. You'll have to stay overnight in a hotel at Heathrow before catching your flight to Trinidad. I'll meet you there. Don't expect any sensational revelations—I don't have any to offer—but I do have a few things to say, about Magdalen, and about Rowland. You won't have to tie yourself in knots trying to conceal the source of the information from Rowland; he's not a fool, and he'll know that I've talked to you. He won't suspect you of being my agent because of it."

"I'm not," I reminded her.

"I know that," she replied. "The important thing is that Rowland knows it too. We'll talk again before you leave."

That was the end of the conversation, for the time being

CHAPTER SIX

Within forty-eight hours, all the loose ends had been tidied up. Not only was the flight to Trinidad booked, but a car had been hired to take me directly to the island's coast, where a boat would be waiting to ferry me all the way to the delta. I was able to call Rowland and give him an estimated time of arrival. We'd already had a discussion about the lab facilities I'd need, in order that we could make a comprehensive list of materials for which we'd have to place orders, and he was now able to tell me that the equipment and supplies he'd ordered would be loaded on to the boat before I reached it. It all seemed slightly surreal, partly because of the pace at which it as all happening, and partly because all the discussion of timetables and equipment orders made it seem as if we were carefully avoiding the real subject of mutual interest—as, indeed, we were.

The train journey from Lancaster to London seemed longer than it ever had before, and even the Heathrow shuttle seemed to take its time, although it was a comparatively short journey. There was no sign of Rosalind when I arrived at the hotel, but I hadn't expected her to be there. She would want to meet in the guaranteed privacy of her own car, not some public building. I'd hardly had time to tidy myself up a little in the room, however, before the call came through summoning me to the lobby again. I recognized the man who was waiting for me there as the petty Saint Peter who'd been manning the gates of Eden during the funeral. He was evidently her rock.

The car that was waiting in the forecourt was a black sedan

with opaque windows—nothing as ostentatious as a limousine. It looked like a glorified taxi, and when I climbed into the back I saw that it did, indeed, have a privacy partition like a taxi. The partition was raised, even though rocks are legendary for their deaf-muteness.

"Thank you for coming, Peter," Rosalind said, although I had been under the impression that I had been the one to demand the information that she was about to impart, or at least dance around. Apparently, she didn't want to cast herself as the proverbial mountain making an improbable concession to some mere mortal who didn't even have a prophet's credentials.

"No problem," I said, and waited. She knew the agenda as well as I did.

For a long moment, however, she was content to look at me, studying me with her gaze. I honestly don't think that she was trying to intimidate me, or to emphasize her authority in any way. She really was studying me, perhaps even wondering whether it really might have made a difference if Magdalen had been prepared to suffer me as a lover, or as a suitor—and whether, if so, there was anything that she might have been able to do to further that eventuality.

In the meantime, the car took off, initially turning south-eastwards along the M25.

When Rosalind finally broke the silence, it was to begin long before what I might have identified as the appropriate beginning. "Do you know why I never had any more sons after Rowland?" she asked.

I figured that she was probably expecting a negative answer, and that the question had only been asked as a prelude to an explanation, but as it happened, I thought that I did know the answer—or, at least, that I could make a guess that wouldn't leave me looking foolish if she had something else in mind. What I actually said, therefore, was: "I believe so."

Her eyes didn't grow wide with astonishment—in fact, they narrowed slightly with suspicion. "What did Rowland tell you?" she asked.

"Nothing," I replied. "In fact, when we talked about the matter, I was the one who initiated the discussion and made the suggestion. I have an interest in those sorts of genetic choices too, remember."

She had probably forgotten, but it only took the slightest of prompts to remind her. "Of course," he said, nodding her head slightly. "Peter Bell the Third. You're part of a scientific dynasty too—but you weren't selected in the same way as my children."

"Not the same way," I confirmed. "My grandfather thought he knew exactly what he was doing, though, when he decided to produce an heir, and so did my father. They could hardly be unaware, given the advancement of genetics and neurology during their lifetimes. They both knew that taking what measures they could to produce a son pre-equipped to be a scientist carried certain risks...and potential penalties. They had their own experiences to draw on, and they both had to justify the decision to go the clonal route. I don't think it ever occurred to either of them that it might be safer to find a wife or a surrogate and produce a daughter instead...or as well. I have no sisters, and no aunts, except on my mother's side."

"Do you regret that?" she was quick to ask.

"Not particularly," I said. "I suppose I did envy Rowland, more than a little, back in the day, and there would have been a certain beautiful symmetry about our little molecule of community if I'd had a sister too...but no, I don't regret it, now."

"That's wise," she said. "Regret is a burden, if not a poison."

The car had already turned off the M25 at the first southward exit, but I didn't imagine for a moment that we were heading for the coast. I assumed that the driver had instructions to follow a vaguely circular course, so that we'd always be within comfortable striking range of Heathrow, able to make a swift return once Rosalind decided that the interview was over.

I didn't attempt to fill the conversational gap. I waited for Rosalind to begin speaking again, and she did. She didn't ask me to fill out what I'd meant by "I believe so"; she was prepared to take the hint from my remarks about my own family history as evidence that I was on the right track…sufficiently, at any rate, for her not to have to spell out her own thinking, which was bound to be afflicted by a measure of uncertainty. Instead, she cut to the chase. "The bond between Rowland and Magdalen was too tight," she said. "I hadn't anticipated that the other circumstances of their planning would affect that. I thought that they'd be much like other pairs of non-identical twins. If anything, I thought the fact that they had different fathers would inhibit their closeness rather than intensifying it. I was wrong."

"I don't think you made any mistakes," I said, quite sincerely. "Nothing culpable, at any rate. There are some things that can't be anticipated. There's always a random factor. The fact that Rowland and Magdalen became as close as they did, and that their closeness worked out in the way that it did, wasn't something you could have anticipated and taken action to prevent. It was just an accident of happenstance."

She didn't bother to thank me for my concern. "What I wish now," she said, "is that they'd been able to follow through—if they'd just got on with it. This is the twenty-second century, damn it. We don't need to be afraid of incest any more. Stupid taboos of that sort can be set aside, now that there's no genetic peril involved. Once she'd decided that she couldn't have you, or anybody else, because of Rowland—however silly that decision was—Magdalen should have had Rowland. Separation, in those circumstances, turned out to be the worst of all worlds. I did urge her to contact you, Peter—and to keep in contact with Rowland too. She did that, after a fashion, but obviously not with any substantial result. I really did do everything I could, Peter—and I need you to make that clear to Rowland. I didn't forbid anything, and I didn't compel anything. All I wanted was for Magadalen—for both of them—to be safe and sane."

She was no longer the perfect model of control she had been when she had summoned me to the Pyramid to receive my orders. I was on board now, doing what she wanted me to do—but she no longer seemed entirely certain what that was, or exactly how I ought to go about it. It was almost as if she were in search of reassurance. Some men might have put out a reassuring hand, and laid it lightly on her wrist, but I was my father's son, shaped to follow in his footsteps as a scientist, just as Rowland and Magdalen had been shaped to follow in Rosalind's. After Rowland, she had not had any more sons, and I knew why.

"I'll do what I can," I promised. "If there's anything I can do to help repair your relationship with Rowland, I'll do it—for his sake. I know that you and I seemed to be on opposite sides, ten years ago, but that was just a by-product of the situation. I don't know what to say to him about Magdalen, though—I don't know what happened, or how, or why."

She pulled herself together then, and fixed me with her artificial stare. "The exact details don't matter," she said. "I suspect Rowland knows more than I do, although I can't be sure. If he wants to know whether I was treating her, yes I was—but not in any drastic way. I prescribed her mild euphorics, nothing more."

"Aether?" I queried. It seemed a natural enough enquiry.

"No," she said, sharply. "I never prescribed Aether."

Not a Hive product, I thought. *The brainchild of someone else's genius.*

"Some of the stuff I persuaded her to take wasn't even real," Rosalind added. "I was hoping for a placebo effect. Love, or lust, or whatever is mostly illusion—if there's one thing in the world that the placebo effect ought to be able to demolish, it's the kind of sickness Magdalen had…but nothing worked. Illusory or not, her trouble was stronger than my ingenuity. Whatever you might have read in the yellow fraction of the web, I'm not really making rapid progress in mind control, with the aid of *fleurs du mal*, and if I were, I certainly wouldn't be testing them on my daughter. I tried to make her feel better—that's all. I failed."

I believed her. Perhaps she regretted, now, that she hadn't tried anything more drastic, but I was prepared to believe that even Rosalind would have taken a gentle and discreet approach to her daughter's unhappiness. Her failure to help must have cut her to the quick; she wasn't used to failure.

"I didn't know whether the treatment would help," she said, "but I was sure that it wouldn't do any harm. I thought it would at least stave off disaster. I really didn't expect to find her dead. If anything, I'd have expected...."

She didn't finish that sentence. At a guess, she'd been about to say that she'd have expected the first and only suicide in the family to be Rowland's, if there were ever to be any at all.

"I'm sorry," I said, offering my condolences for the fact that Rosalind had not only failed to save her daughter, even by means of subtle trickery, but had been the one to find her dead. I didn't know what else to say. I didn't know that there was anything else I could say.

If I'd had to offer my own hypothesis about Magdalen's suicide I would have guessed that Magdalen had committed suicide because of a sense of desolation that she couldn't shake off by any means, including Rosalind's pychotropics and placebos. She had felt that sense of desolation, I estimated, because she couldn't be with Rowland, but felt that that she couldn't be with anyone else either, because of Roland, and had felt, in the end, that she couldn't bear to be alone either. Sometimes, sisterhood isn't enough, no matter how highly developed it might be. Guessing all that and knowing it, however, were two different things. I hadn't seen or spoken to Magdalen in years. What did I know? Wasn't I just projecting from what I'd observed when we were all a good deal younger? Perhaps Magdalen had changed in the interim. I hadn't, but perhaps she had. I didn't have any right to offer hypotheses to Rosalind—so I kept quiet. I just kept quiet.

A few moments ago, I'd been surprised that Rosalind had suddenly seemed human, for once in her life. Now, she seemed very human indeed—more so than me, in fact. I felt profoundly uncomfortable.

"I need to know that Rowland's all right," she said. "He doesn't have to talk to me, if he doesn't want to, but I need to know that he's all right. He's my son."

I could have told her, yet again, that I would do what I could, but she already knew that, and the promise was effectively empty while neither of us knew what I might be able to do. I couldn't believe, any longer, that she was here in order that I could be more fully informed when I had to answer Rowland's questions. She was in search of something else, and probably didn't know what it was. Neither did I.

She didn't say anything more, though. She looked at me, still probing for an opportunity to meet my eyes. It was my turn; she wanted me to take the conversational initiative—but I had no idea what to say. I glanced out of the window, noting that the setting sun was now to the left of the car's course and deducing that we had turned northwards, somewhere in the rural wilds of western Surrey or eastern Hampshire, but the dusk seemed gloomier than usual because of the tinted windows and the landscape was too vague to allow precise identification.

Rosalind took the glance, and my consequent expression, as a hint. She switched on the light. Her brass-blonde hair and piercing blue eyes seemed to flare up and intensify their beauty. Rowland, who had rarely descended so far as to refer to his mother as "the Queen Bee," had sometimes referred to her, just between the two of us, as Ayesha—knowing that I could and would translate that as She-Who-Must-Be-Obeyed.

She was still waiting for me to talk. Wherever the car was, it wasn't skirting the runways at Heathrow. Eventually, I talked.

"My father was a scientist through and through," I said. "A physicist, like his father before him, not a namby-pamby biologist. A *solid-state* physicist…and in person, a man of very solid state. He'd probably heard the name Shelley, but he'd never read a poem in his life, and probably wouldn't have been able to grasp its meaning if he had. He named me in all innocence."

That broke through her mental blockade efficiently enough. She had little alternative but to raise her stately eyebrows and say: "What on earth are you talking about?"

"There's a poem by Shelley called 'Peter Bell the Third,' which is a parody of a poem by Wordsworth called 'The Tale of Peter Bell.' Wordsworth's poem is about a potter who goes off the rails but is redeemed by an encounter with a supernatural ass—a literal donkey, not a metaphorical one. Wordsworth though it was a masterpiece, but other people—including Shelley—thought it was absurd. There's a possibility that Wordsworth might have had Shelley in mind when he wrote the poem, Shelley's initials being P. B., or, at least, that Shelley might have thought so. Shelley's reply is about a posthumous Peter Bell and his misadventures in Hell. It's quite amusing—unless your name happens, coincidentally, to be Peter Bell the Third, in which case the sarcasm takes on a considerably sharper edge, and one or two of the insults become decidedly offensive."

Rosalind thought about that for a moment or two, and then said: "So you understand about the Usher thing, then?"

"Yes," I said.

I did understand about "the Usher thing," and why it might add measurably to the embarrassment, if not the tragedy, of two siblings tempted to incest, whether they resisted the temptation or not. That was what I was trying to get across to her.

She took my word for it, and nodded. "I thought it was harmless," Rosalind told me. "After all, I didn't call Rowland Roderick, and I didn't call Magdalen Madeleine. I thought the faint echo was harmless—and I was always slightly disapproving of Daddy's effective rejection of the name, on what seemed to me to be silly grounds. I hadn't realized that you were similarly afflicted…but I suppose it's not that uncommon, given the sheer abundance of the English literary legacy. There can't be many people around whose names *haven't* been pre-echoed in some stupid story—and given the nature of stories, few of the echoes are likely to be flattering. We're not dealing with curses, though. There's no *causality* here."

"No solid-state physical causality," I agreed. "But you understand the placebo effect as well as anyone."

Her blue eyes seemed actually to become brighter as that thrust struck home, and I realized that, for once in her life, Rosalind really wasn't in control. The blaze in her eyes was just an illusion, though.

I hadn't even meant what I'd said. It had just been wordplay. Eddie Poe had had no more effect on Magdalen than Percy Shelley had had on me. There was no metaphorical placebo effect in operation. There was no pseudocausal link at all in any echo there might have been in Magdalen Usher's fate to that of any imaginary predecessor, any more than there was any pseudocausal link between Percy Shelley's *jeu d'esprit* and any sensation I might ever have had, or still might have, that I was living in Hell and eternally damned. In both cases, it was purely and simply a matter of the effects of unrequited love—a cliché so old that it had been "pre-echoed" a million times over in life and literature alike.

I wondered whether Rosalind was really capable of under-standing what had happened to Magdalen, given that she had probably never experienced unrequited love herself...unless you counted her love for Rowland in that category. Could I be certain, though, that she hadn't ever loved anyone in the utterly hopeless fashion that Magdalen had loved Rowland? Rosalind's life-story, as I knew it, gave the impression of someone who had never had the slightest romantic interest in anyone, but publicly-available life-stories can sometimes be deceptive, even when they seem to make sense. What did anyone actually know, after all, about the intimate life of Elizabeth I? And Rosalind did make sense. No matter what other criticisms could be leveled against her, she certainly made sense.

"You need to be careful," Rosalind said to me, returning to the nub of the matter, "in what you say to Rowland, and how. I've told you what little I can about Magdalen's death, and—more importantly—I've told you what I don't know. I can guess, you can guess, and Rowland will guess too—but at the end of the day, we don't know. We never can and never will."

That was true, in a strictly logical sense.

"I'll be careful," I promised.

"If I thought I could do this myself, you know, I would," she told me, unnecessarily. "If I thought one of his sisters...but such is the cruelty of circumstance that we could only make matters worse. You're the only one who can help him, if he does need help. The only person in the world."

I wasn't at all sure that I *could* help, if Rowland really was in need of help, but I was fairly sure that I wouldn't make things worse—and I tended to agree with Rosalind that she, or any one of her many surviving daughters, might have made things worse, if they'd tried to force themselves upon him.

"I'll do my best," I promised.

She was still looking at me, still studying me. Perhaps she had learned more from our brief encounter than I had. She'd never bothered to study me before, when I was only Rowland's friend, even though she knew by then how difficult Rowland found it to make friends.

"I do wish things had worked out differently," she said, in a tone tinged with wonderment. She had always had such control over her life and surroundings that she had never been able to see herself as a victim of circumstances. Now she knew regret, as a burden and a poison. She had more than dozen other daughters, but that didn't reconcile her in the least to the fact that she no longer had Magdalen, and now had to live with the suspicion that if only she'd done things differently—if only she'd known what to do differently—things might have worked out differently.

"So do I," I said, as blandly as I could.

CHAPTER SEVEN

I wouldn't have got much sleep in any case, knowing that I had to get up at five-thirty to check in on my room's web-console and then get over to the terminal in time to board. I would have been on edge even if I hadn't had that bizarre conversation with Rosalind in her blacked-out car, or even if we'd actually spelled out more of what we had to say rather than leaving so much to inference—but there are things that are difficult to say aloud, especially in an era that prides itself on its New Privacy. Although the conventions of the New Privacy had initially been designed as defenses against web leakage, they had inevitably spread their tentacles far and wide.

Eugenics is one of those things that, in the modern world, everybody likes to practice but nobody likes to talk about. It carries too much historical and literary baggage. Rosalind had probably been profoundly glad when I told her that I understood, without it being spelled out, why she had had no more sons after Rowland—and why, as a pre-corollary of the same concern—Roderick the Great had elected to leave his own heritage to a daughter, rather than a son.

Back in the twentieth century, when practical eugenics first became feasible, thanks to *in vitro* fertilization and the selection of eggs and sperms, even the word "eugenics" had been taboo, and nobody ever used it to describe what they were doing when people carrying seriously problematic genes made certain that the particular eggs and sperms employed to create their offspring were free of those hazards. It must have been obvious, even then, that as reproductive technologies continued to improve, and understanding of genetic potentials improved in tandem, the choices available would become increasingly complex. Even before the advent of the twenty-first century, there were sperm-donor banks in existence that selected for intelligence, athletic ability, musical talent and a score of other factors, to the rough-and-ready extent that it could then be done. And by that time, people had known for centuries, if only as an item of crude folk wisdom, that "genius" and "madness" were closely and strangely allied.

Strictly speaking, that isn't true—but when it did become possible to speak more strictly, to define more exactly what was going on in neurological terms when individuals had a natural aptitude for mathematics, painting or gymnastics, the alliance between the closeness and the strangeness only became more intricate and more challenging. It had then become possible to found a proper academic discipline of practical neurology, but the art had been in its infancy when Rowland and I had taken Professor Fliegmann's pioneering course at Imperial.

In themselves, of course, genes don't "cause" physical characteristics. What they do is make proteins. Even the "control genes" making proteins that determine when and where other genes are switched on in various specialized tissues don't cause anything in a crudely deterministic sense—but they do help to create propensities on which experience of the world, education and rigorous training can work. Innate talents and character defects still have to be nurtured or opposed, developed and shaped by culture and effort, but they do exist, and they don't materialize at random, even though the paths of facilitation are sometimes hard to detect. There are random factors involved, as there are in any complex system, but that doesn't affect the fact that there are fundamental patterns, which usually survive any amount of supplementary random noise.

Sometime around the end of the twentieth century, it was discovered that mathematical ability and the scientific mind-set were based in the enhanced activity of certain parts of the brain, and the particular patterns of initial neural connection present in those areas. The propensity in question begins development in the embryo, prior to birth, in response to a complex combination of factors, some directly genetic and some "indirectly genetic," in the sense that the effect is hormonally mediated. One of the most significant phases in the chain of causality occurs in the seventh month of pregnancy, when hormonal releases in the body trigger the changes determining whether an individual embryo will manifest male or female secondary sexual characteristics. In the vast majority of cases, of course, the former are chromosomally XY and the latter XX, but there are exceptions and anomalies—and, of course, degrees of effect, even in the cases where the pattern is sustained.

Nobody was a hundred-per-cent sure, back at the dawn of the twenty-first century, whether "secondary sexual characteristics" included mental tendencies, although ninety-nine per cent of the people who took a guess figured that they did, and that the fact that almost all the mathematical and musical geniuses of the past had been male wasn't simply a reflection of the way that boys and girls had been brought up. Once the genes influencing brain development, both directly and indirectly, had been identified, and sophisticated technological control of the hormonal activity of embryos became possible, the possibility of selecting children for all kinds of talents and potentialities became possible.

In the short term, of course, it led to certain demographic distortions, much as the advent of sex-selection had initially led to a large preponderance of male births—but such distortions tend to be self-correcting, partly because shortages of supply lead to increases in perceived economic value, and partly because intense competition in producing particular results tends to highlight the hazards associated with such results. From an objective viewpoint, however, one couldn't say that a large number of parents wanting smarter and more scientifically-inclined children was a bad thing, given that the ecocatastrophe was already turning into the Crash. If ever the world had needed scientific geniuses by the score, that was the time. One might almost suspect the involvement of the hand of Providence, especially if you believe that it's the crafty kind of hand that never gives without taking something away…but I digress.

The first role of genetic engineering is that you can never do just one thing. Genes are multifunctional; you can't produce one result without producing others, and an attempted increase in one result inevitable leads to increases in the others, not necessarily in proportion. Something else people had known for centuries before the Crash, glimpsed through the clouded lens of crude folk wisdom, was that great mathematicians and scientists, and great musicians and artists, tended to pay a penalty for their exceptionality in terms of other facets of the personality. They were not "mad," in the sense that they were subject to some kind of mental "illness," but their minds tended to work in particular and peculiar ways that, if exaggerated, tended toward what was once called "autism." Crudely put, born scientists were often potentially brilliant in terms of limited focus, but anything but brilliant when it came to functioning efficiently in a social environment. Some mathematical geniuses and brilliant painters were unable even to communicate with other people with any degree of comfort or efficacy.

For a while, it was thought that there might be single spectrum of bundled functions and dysfunctions, which began with "normal" female behavior and then extended through "normal" male behavior and various kinds of "genius" to the breakdown point of "autism," but that inevitably turned out to be far too simple as a scheme of conceptual geometry. There was an axis of sorts there, but it was complicated by all kinds of extensions into other dimensions—far more than three of them. By the time sophisticated mapping of the propensities became possible, it required a clever AI or a highly unusual genius to get anywhere near a capacity to "visualize" its conceptual geometry—but it could be done, mathematically.

When Peter Bell the First and Roderick the Great decided that they wanted their children to be chips off the old block—scientists of very considerable ability, if not of genius—that kind of practical neurology was still in its relative infancy, but it could be done, to a reasonable level of approximation. Satisfaction was pretty much guaranteed, in the ability department, and the hazards could—in theory at least—be minimized. Where the acceptable minimum was located was, of course, a matter of opinion.

Peter Bell the First took the straightforward option, and decided that his son and heir ought to be a biological clone—which minimized some of the risks, but by no means all. The very making of that choice, however, illustrated the fact that he possessed one of the frequent corollaries of scientific genius that some people might regard as a dysfunction: he was subject to an intense feeling of superiority, which made him construe his failures to relate successfully to other human beings as a reflection of their incompetence rather than his. To sum the situation up with brutal simplicity, he was an arrogant son-of-a-bitch, who was very efficient in his vocation, and won awards for that reason, but whom nobody actually liked—including, as it turned out, and perhaps especially, his own clone, Peter Bell the Second.

Roderick the Great was a subtler thinker by far than Peter Bell the First. He had observed the difficulties that often afflicted great scientists in relationships with other human beings, including their own children, and had taken due note of the number of sons of scientists who deliberately chose to direct their efforts in a direction entirely different to the ones their fathers had taken, sometimes refusing to extend their intellectual potential at all. Perhaps because he was a biologist, and not a physical scientist, Roderick made a far more intensive study of practical neurology *per se*, and came up with the theory that that a male scientist who wanted a reliable heir would do far better to have a female child, who might be unlikely to exhibit the desirable qualities of scientific genius to quite the same degree as a male, but would also be far less likely to suffer the consequences of the undesirable ones. Hence Rosalind, who did not hate Roderick as Peter Bell the Second had hated Peter Bell the First, but loved him very dearly, and did indeed set out to carry forward his intellectual dynasty exactly as he would have wished.

Way beyond the effects of genetics, there is a momentum in such multigenerational processes, of which Rosalind was a beneficiary—and how! The rise of the new house of Usher not only continued, but accelerated, and became unstoppable. That was one in the eye for Eddie Poe—who had, of course, been innocent of any malicious intent in plucking a name out of the air to bestow upon the luckless protagonist of "The Fall of the House of Usher." On the other hand, it wasn't entirely obvious that Rosalind had entirely avoided the pitfalls so often associated with male scientific genius.

And so to the second generation.

Peter Bell the Second's hatred of his father did not take the form of differentiation, as it might easily have done, but of competition. He did not shun solid-state physics, but threw himself into it with a whole heart, intent on surpassing and superseding his parent's discoveries. Did he succeed? The scientific jury is, I believe, still out. In any case, my father is still alive, so the game is still in play, and will not be over until the Grim Reaper comes to call for a second time—which, given the present state of medical capability, might not be for a long time. My father has already scored one significant victory in outliving his model and rival, so I presume that he must be reckoned to have taken the lead—but we haven't spoken for years, and I'm no physicist, so I'm not sure exactly how their positions stand, in a purely scientific context.

The dysfunctional fever of arrogant competition being what it is, Peter Bell the Second was always going to produce a clone, and he was always going to do his utmost to make sure that his clone didn't follow the same path of fierce hatred that his father's clone had done. By the time he got around to the task of self-reproduction, ectogenetic technology had made numerous significant advances, so he had a better physiological armory at his disposal for the purposes of embryological direction and control. Whether he directed its use wisely, I am not the person to judge, but he does seem to have succeeded in making sure that I would not be the diehard rival to his accomplishments that he was to his father's. My scientific proclivities were always orientated in a different direction, and I think that my father was glad, although perhaps not wholeheartedly, when he eventually found out that he had spawned a geneticist.

Was he successful in the other aspect of his ambition? I think he was, but I can see how others might beg to disagree. I don't believe that I hate my father, and would say, if pressed, that I am utterly indifferent to him. On the other hand, I certainly do not love him—and, as I said, I haven't spoken to him in years. It would not trouble me unduly if I never spoke to him again, but I will go to his funeral, if and when the occasion arises. I owe him that much—and probably a good deal more, though nothing for which I feel particularly grateful.

I never had a mother, of course, so the fact that I never loved my father means that the only person I have ever loved, and perhaps ever will love, is, or was, Magdalen Usher—but I am not the object of this lesson, and am merely present within it to illustrate a general principle and its variations. The real point of the exercise, you will doubtless remember, is why Rosalind only ever had one son, but a multitude of daughters.

Rosalind was her father's daughter. Had her father not died while she was still relatively young—prematurely, in today's terms, although the fallout of the Crash was still rather unsettled thirty years ago—he might have taken a more active role in guiding her reproduction. He did die, though, and Rosalind was not content simply to echo his own choice, especially as the dramatic end of the perceived population crisis liberated her to think in terms of more than one child. Perhaps, in some sense, she could not be content to echo his choice, because she felt a powerful desire, if not an actual need, to replace him. At any rate, she decided that she would have a son, and a son of genius, but that she would try to compensate for the dysfunctions that might be attendant upon that genius by providing him with an intimate social relationship that would provide him with a private arena in which to learn and practice social skills, by giving him a near-twin half-sister.

I might well be insulting Rosalind by putting the calculation in those cold terms. I probably sound sarcastic, but if I do, that has more to do with my psychological situation than hers. I don't intend to imply that Rosalind did what she did for a bad reason. I have every reason to believe that she loves all her children very dearly—even the one who is no longer alive. I'm not suggesting that she had anything but the very best of intentions in trying to maximize Rowland's and Magadalen's chances of a happy and successful life. Yes, it was, in retrospect, a recipe for intense incestuous feelings that were perhaps always more likely to end in confusion and disaster than any mere sin, but that was not what she wanted. What she wanted was a boy who might equal Roderick, in more ways than one—and at the very least, she was too wise by far to think that the best route to that outcome would be to clone her father. She was a geneticist, not a physicist; she knew where the limits of genetic practicality lay.

Did Rowland break her heart? No, I don't believe so. Was he a thankless child, a metaphorical serpent's tooth? No, not that either. I don't believe that Rowland is indifferent to his mother, as I am to my father; I believe that he loves her—but he has, as people are wont to say in Lancashire "a funny way of showing it."

Having replaced Roderick, Rosalind did not see the need to repeat the gesture, and was content to follow Roderick's thesis that female children were more likely to be successful in life as well as science, by virtue of the moderation of their anti-social tendencies.

Perhaps I am being too vague here in spelling out the "dysfunctions" frequently associated with the scientific mind-set. As I said before, it has nothing to do with "mental illness," and is primarily concerned with the relationship between sensation and cognition. That is what the scientific mind-set *is*, in essence: a particular relationship between sensation and cognition, which is inclined toward obsessive attention, disciplined observation, habitual analysis and complex theorization. It is, in a purely logical sense, not easily compatible with empathy. There is more than one alternative mind-set, and the scientific mind-set is capable of more detailed categorization, but in general, the alternative mind-sets typical of the human brain have various features in common. Many people automatically meet the gaze of others; those possessed of the scientific mindset often have to make a conscious effort to do so. Many people automatically respond sympathetically to touch; those possessed of the scientific mind-set often have to make a conscious effort even to tolerate it, no matter how much they might desire it.

Such factors can make friendship difficult, let alone love—but they are not matters of conscious decision. The defective lens of folk wisdom often used to represent possessors of the scientific mind-set as cold, unfeeling people, perhaps even incapable of emotion. That is not the case; there is nothing sociopathic, psychopathic, schizoid or paranoid about the mind-set itself, although scientists are as vulnerable as anyone else to the random predations of diseases that generate mental symptoms. In general, possessors of the scientific mind-set are by no means unemotional; it is simply that they channel and express their emotions in different ways. They tend to be more extreme and less mutable in their affections. If they do not make friends easily, they maintain bonds of friendship very firmly, even in the absence of everyday reinforcement. If they do not fall in love easily, they tend to do so heavily and cripplingly, even in the absence of what people with different mind-sets consider to the customary expressions and manifestations of love.

That, at least, is how I see the situation—although people possessed of different mind-sets might find it odd, or even incomprehensible.

Not all people possessed of a scientific mind-set are scientists, of course; there are all kinds of reasons why they might divert their efforts into different vocations. Although most litterateurs are, as is only to be expected, possessed of empathic mind-sets, some benefit from the tendencies of the analytical mindset—Edgar Allan Poe and Percy Bysshe Shelley, to name but two. Either of those men, had he been inclined or able to make the choice, might have been a great scientist instead of a great poet. Some scientists, at least, might have been great poets had they taken a different direction in life, although I am not the person to judge whether I might have been one of them. Rowland could have, I think. Perhaps Magdalen should have, if only to free herself from Eden and the Hive. We are no long living in the nineteenth century, though. What scope and demand is there for poets nowadays?

As for Rosalind, I am obliged to conclude, in spite of the fact that I do not really like the woman, that she really was a successful product of Roderick's genius. She is not only a great scientist but a great artist too. Her understanding of beauty might be based in a scientific mind-set, but she does understand beauty and she is a prolific creator of beauty. Her understanding of eroticism is similarly based in analysis and theorization, but she does understand it, and her mastery of olfactory psychotropics is no mere chemistry. I know little or nothing about her love life, but everything I do know inclines me to believe that she is an exceptional human being in every respect—which makes it all the more remarkable, in a way, that she neither foresaw nor was able to prevent her daughter's premature death. But even perfect human beings have flaws—how could they be perfect if they had not, given that humanity is, in essence, flawed?

Even Peter Bell the First—whose arrogance was, I would like to believe, far greater than my own—knew that humanity has intrinsic flaws. He was more prepared to tolerate his own flaws than other people's—but aren't we all?

Rosalind knew regret, now, as burden and poison. I had known it for a long time, as Rowland had—but evidently not as dolorously, or at least not as decisively, as Magdalen.

I was still sure, even as my plane touched down in Trinidad, that my going to visit Rowland could not and would not do him any harm. I wanted to see him. He wanted to see me. There really were unique opportunities in the Orinoco delta for studying the crisis-reactions of algal species. But still, in spite of all of that, there was something deep within me—something deep within my scientific mind-set—that kept telling me that I shouldn't have gone to Magdalen's funeral, that I shouldn't have exposed myself to Rosalind's grief and Rosalind's need.

The first and foremost thing of which scientists are always acutely aware is the need to remain objective, external to the phenomena under consideration. The second is that it's impossible to meet that need. No matter how inconvenient it is, we are in the world and part of the phenomena. I shouldn't have gone to the funeral, but I had to. There was no alternative. I had to meet Rosalind's grief, and Rosalind's need. I had to come to see Rowland, not just for my sake and for his, but for Rosalind's, and Magdalen's Magadalen was dead; she had presumably killed herself in order to be free of her own insatiable, ineradicable need—but the rest of us weren't free of it, and never would be, while we were still alive.

CHAPTER EIGHT

Eddie Poe would doubtless have been delighted to know that it was a dull, dark and seemingly-soundless day on which I finally approached the remarkable house that my friend Rowland Usher had built, in the loneliest spot he could find, in the new wilderness of the regenerated Orinoco delta. I say *seemingly-soundless* because I was being ferried there by a boat with a powerful internal-combustion engine, and the stuttering growl of that engine was all too evident. Its very insistence, however, emphasized that it was alien to the scene, and that without its rude interruption, the delta would indeed have been silent.

In the olden days, before the sea had made its fatal incursion and mounted its subsequent retreat, there would have been plenty of sounds. The hum of insects would not have extended so far over the water, but the calls of birds would have done so, and perhaps the occasional cry of a jaguar. There would certainly have been distant sounds of some kind of human activity. Now, though, the birds were only just beginning to return, and were still maintaining a mute discretion, jaguars were extinct and other mammals would take a great deal longer to put in an appearance. As for the humans…well, the humans were as unpredictable as ever, but they had not yet started making a noise.

The morning was dull and dark because the sky was covered in sullen cloud, behind which the invisible sun was already setting, signifying its presence by a dull ruddy glow that seemed more sulky than fiery. The clouds gave the impression that they were trying to rain, but had not quite summoned up the energy. We were still in the "rainy season," although its peak had passed.

I had been traveling for more than twenty-four hours—which had been transformed into twenty-eight by the clock—but I was neither unduly tired not unduly disorientated. I had slept unusually well on the plane, and the tropical air seemed strangely invigorating. I felt awake and energized.

I was studying the placid surface of the water rather than the uneasy condition of the sky. A layman would have seen it as mottled green and curiously slimy, and might even have thought it stagnant, given the stillness of the moment, but I knew more than enough about algae to know that it was a far-from-stagnant battleground, where the flow of the numerous branches of the mighty river and the tides of the mightier ocean maintained incessantly shifting fronts and conflicts, creating ever-fluid challenges to freshwater specialists and saltwater specialists, and golden opportunities for versatile species that could adapt to and exploit vagaries in salinity. There was abundant fish-food there, but not, as yet, abundant fish to make use of it. Like the birds, the fish were coming back, but tentatively. Unlike the birds, the fish were capable of sudden population explosions, but conditions were not sufficiently settled, as yet, to permit or facilitate such explosions.

The mottled green surface was, in consequence, not merely interesting to me but beautiful in its intricacy and its complex implication.

The boat's captain could not share my aesthetic appreciation or my fascination, but he was not surprised by it. He knew Rowland, because he ferried deliveries to Rowland's home on a regular basis. He doubtless thought that Rowland was "mad," and that any friend of Rowland's was virtually certain to be "mad" as well.

Fortunately, I didn't have to make conversation with the captain, as his English was a trifle rudimentary and my Spanish even worse. Although he and his boat were resident in Trinidad, he was descended from refugees. His grandfather, if not his father, had been Venezuelan—and the boat certainly seemed old enough to have belonged to his grandfather, although it had doubtless undergone numerous repairs and refits in the interim. He had probably clung to his grandfather's language as a means of asserting his roots, and perhaps expressing a vague intention of one day "coming home."

Although we weren't in conversation, I noticed the captain watching me when Rowland's "house" first came into view and I raised my eyes to study it. He probably expected me to say: "What's that?"—or at least to make some remark about its bizarre nature. I didn't, even though the pictures I'd seen didn't do it justice, not just because it had grown in the interim, but because there as a wealth of fine detail visible to the naked eye that the photographic images hadn't captured.

Rosalind had described Rowland's house as a "glorified termite mound," but she had been thinking about its eccentric construction techniques rather than its appearance. In terms of its fundamental shape, it was not so very different from the Great Pyramid of Eden; it was approximately the same height, square-ish at the base, with four sloping faces. It had fewer windows, especially in its lower reaches, and more eccentric protrusions, which included the usual balconies, gargoyles and communication masts but also a considerable number of organic nodes and spikes with no obvious function. Some of them looked like thorns, and others not unlike flowers—but the latter were more like heraldic roses than the natural kind.

One of the edifice's four faces was equipped at the base with a sizeable walled harbor, where three boats of various were moored and there was room for two more of similar size to the ferry. I could understand why a simple jetty couldn't have done the job, having studied the weather reports for the region. Fortunately, I had arrived too late in the year to catch anything more than the autumnal end of the hurricane season, but that didn't mean that I wouldn't have the chance to see a spectacular storm or two, and a good deal of heavy rain. The sea might have retreated somewhat, but the atmosphere was still considerably warmer and more violent than its pre-Crash average.

Beyond the stone jetty that ran along the front of the house there were three doors, two them as large as coaching entrances, presumably giving access to warehouses. The one in the middle, which presumably gave access to the stairways and elevators leading to the upper floors of the house, was conspicuously modest, but also conspicuously armored in steel. I couldn't imagine that anyone was ever likely to try to rob the house, but Rowland obviously believed in not taking any chances. He was, after all, living in a region devoid of law, or even of civilization.

Apart from the artificial harbor, the house was surrounded by water, although there were huge, epiphyte-laden mangroves growing in a semi-circular arc behind it, and spurs of land decked with palms and other trees extending raggedly from both horns of the semicircle. The setting was vaguely reminiscent of a shallow lagoon about two hundred meters in diameter, surrounded to a extent of about three hundred degrees by a coral atoll—but the remaining sixty degrees that was open to the broad waters of the river and the tides of the sea provided a vast gateway for vessels like the ferry, which was able to steer directly for the harbor entrance without its pilot having to worry about underwater hazards. I knew that lagoons were supposed to be atypical of the delta, whose channels had been unusually disciplined in olden days, but it was difficult to discern, as yet, whether the restored delta would retain all its old characteristics.

My gaze inevitably tilted upwards as we drew closer to the edifice. By the time we came into the harbor it was looming up into the sky like a multicolored mountain, without a definite angle anywhere in spite of its discernible faces. Unlike the tip of the Great Pyramid of Eden, Roland's house did not come to a point, but was rounded off, although the edges of the rounded hump were decorated with uneven crenellations—the merest suggestion of battlements—and a number of subsidiary projections, only a few of which included gutters to project water away from the walls.

Rowland was waiting on the quayside, having doubtless seen the boat approaching while it was still some distance away. There were two other people with him—a male and a female clad, as he was, in long-sleeved white shirts and khaki trousers, and wearing large straw hats. Their faces were dark, though, while Rowland's seemed uncannily pale, hardly touched by the sun at all. My own face must have seemed equally foreign in its pallor—I too was wearing a broad-brimmed hat to keep my face in the shade and a long-sleeved shirt to protect my arms. I knew from experience, however, that after two or three expeditions in search of specimens, the color of my skin would begin to turn bronze. Either Rowland did not get out much, or his skin was reluctant to produce melanin.

Even as the boat was still approaching, and neither of us thought that it was close enough as yet to make it worth shouting a greeting, I saw that I had definitely been wrong about Rowland's phone using an unvarnished camera-image. Not only did he look considerably paler than he had in the image, but thinner and somehow more agitated. I put the seeming agitation due to excitement at the prospect of seeing me again after so many years, but I was by no means certain of that diagnosis. He did not look well.

Greetings were exchanged, however, with a suitable flux of enthusiasm. The boat had a crew of four, and its captain was not averse to pitching in, so there were nine of us to help with the unloading of the vessel, but there was only one gangplank and no cranes or pulleys, so the job took time and we all seemed to spend a great deal of time standing aside to let someone else cross over between deck and shore. When we were done, though, Rowland sent one of his companions—whom he had introduced, perhaps jokingly, as Adam and Eve—to fetch a case full of bottles from a refrigerator in one of the store-rooms. There was beer for the boat's crewmen, but I followed the example of Rowland and his helpers in preferring iced water.

I was sweating profusely; I knew that it would take me several days, at least, to adjust to the ambient outdoor temperature. I had already had enough tropical heat to make me hope with all my heart that Rowland's peculiar dwelling had adequate air-conditioning.

It wasn't until the boat pulled away from the quayside again and chugged through the harbor entrance, homeward bound for Trinidad, that Rowland and I loosened up sufficiently to talk.

"You look well," Rowland commented. "Don't try to tell me that I do too—I know how I look. I'm not ill, but I might have been overdoing things slightly, and my mind's been in turmoil since I heard the news." While speaking he moved indoors, leaving Adam and Eve to tidy up on the quay, and closed the door behind us.

"Only to be expected," I murmured. "I hope you'll be able to take a little time away from your obsessions, now that my presence gives you a duty of hospitality, as well as providing an excuse."

As I had expected, the vestibule within the doorway was equipped with two elevators, as well as entrances to at least three stairways—I say *at least* because there were two closed doors, which might also have given access to staircases, although it seemed more likely that they were closets. There was also a portal giving access to a sloping ramp, which appeared to initiate a spiral corridor winding around the interior of pyramid. We took one of the elevators.

"Of course I'll take time out when I can," Rowland said, "unless you're so eager to hurl yourself into your own research that you have no time for me."

"Don't worry," I said. "My routine's been well and truly broken. I saw J. V. Crowthorne at the funeral, by the way. He asked after you, inevitably."

"How is he?" Rowland asked. "Still tweaking tree-genes to produce more easily workable wood?"

"Apparently," I said. "He doesn't look a day older than he did ten years ago—but most people don't, nowadays. Except for the young, of course, who are still maturing—which includes us."

"Does it?" he said, but was quick to add: "I suppose it does.

If these new nanotechnologies really can extend the lifespan to two or three hundred years, I suppose even octogenarians might count themselves adolescents, let alone septuagenarians. Speaking of septuagenarians...."

"Yes," I said, "I've seen Rosalind. Twice, in fact. Once at the funeral, once at the airport. We had quite a long chat, on the second occasion. She sends her love."

"You must thank her kindly for that, when you get back," he said, with deliberate laconism.

The elevator was still moving—quite slowly, I thought, although it wasn't easy to estimate. The buttons weren't numbered; nor were they arranged in a single vertical line. They were, however, color coded. They were grouped into a triangular array with a spike; there were four black buttons, three white, two red, one blue, one yellow and one green. The green one was at the top of the array; that was the one that Rowland had pressed.

"You could have called her," I pointed out to Rowland, "at least to offer your condolences. You still can."

He didn't make any explicit reply, but he muttered something as if to himself, and I thought I caught the phrase "can of worms." I gathered that he was afraid of what a resumption of communication with his mother might lead to. There was a further question trembling on his lips but he didn't want to ask it in an elevator. When the doors opened he drew me along a corridor that curved around to the left quite sharply. There were doors to either side at regular intervals. He paused at the fourth on the right to say: "This will be your bedroom, if that's okay." He opened the door to show me a room that looked like a standard hotel room, with an *en suite* bathroom, but didn't go in. "Adam will bring your personal luggage up," he added. "You might need to help him install the lab equipment you ordered, though."

"I hope my presence doesn't make too much extra work for your staff," I said. "I'm very self-sufficient—I don't need much in the way of service."

"Don't worry," he said. "Adam and Eve aren't quite sure whether they're in Heaven or Hell here, but they know when they're well off. They were both orphaned by the latter phases of the Crash, although it was admirable that their parents managed to stay alive as long as they did. They put it down to their Indian blood, but there are no more native tribesmen left in Venezuela, any more than the Caribbean islands. They're probably descended from maroons—but that doesn't affect their sense of homeland."

"Are they husband and wife?" I asked.

"In effect," he said. "They haven't been through any public ceremony, but with no community to organize one…that's presumably why they decided to call themselves Adam and Eve when I took them on…although it's possible that thy didn't have any confidence, in the beginning, in my ability to pronounce whatever names they had before. They have no children, though—a source of some sorrow, but it's nothing I can correct. Eve's problem, alas."

Considering how Cain and Abel worked out, I thought, *it might have been better if the original Adam and Eve hadn't bothered.*

"This is my bedroom, here on the left," Rowland put in, before continuing his train of thought. "Their English is reasonably good, even though they only talk to one another in some weird quasi-Spanish dialect that I can hardly follow." Then he changed tack again to say: "You're still a bachelor, I assume?"

"Yes," I said, curtly, as he opened a further door, into what I instantly labeled a study, although I could equally well have called it a library. It had six big screens, three of them equipped with consoles, but Rowland was not the kind of man to do all his reading on screen. There were decks of long shelves along two of the walls, containing at least four hundred books, mostly pre-Crash, as well as cases full of memory-sticks of various kinds. There wasn't much blank wall-space, because there was a broad set of French windows letting out on to a balcony, but the two considerable spaces that did remain were taken up by huge intimate pictures of flowers, if not by Georgia O'Keefe herself, then by some recent imitator. They were actual paintings, not prints, although they might have been copies rather than originals.

"Sure," he said, as my gaze moved slowly over the paintings, one at a time, "Rosalind would be delighted to think...or to believe...that I've inherited her taste in art. I keep the family pictures in the bedroom—including hers. This is where I pass most of my leisure time...it hasn't seen as much use recently as it should have, I expect we'll be spending more time here in future."

He waved a negligent arm at a pair of armchairs situated in the angle where the book-laden walls met. One of them looked brand new, or at least unused. Taking his negligent wave as an invitation, I sat down in the new one, while he went to a sideboard and poured us two drinks from a decanter—iced water again, although he took care to put a slice of lemon in this time.

"Local lemons?" I asked.

"Home-grown," he assured me. "Everything fresh is home-grown, in a perfectly literal sense. We have a small kitchen-garden at the back of the house, and half a dozen plantations of various kinds on the shore—but they're all grafted on to the house's extending roots, all extensions of it. In time, the house will begin to displace the rain forest with its own substance. The grafted fruit and vegetable stocks all do very well, in spite of the rain and the heat. They're Roderick's finest, guaranteed pest-immune, and their specialist pollinators love it here. It's a new kind of Eden, from the fruit-trees' viewpoint, and using the house's roots rather than their own adds a new order of magnitude to their strength and resilience. I envy them, sometimes... but it's the natural destiny of animals, especially humans, to be essentially rootless, parasites in our homes rather than parts of them. So—for the present, at least—all of our meat's tissue-cultured. The only animal husbandry going on inside the house is concerned with insects. I don't eat insects, even though some of them are perfectly edible. It would be too vulgar."

I was glad to hear that speech, because it was the Rowland I knew, quintessentially. That kind of imaginative extravagance, spiced with eccentric wit, was what I had loved most about him, in the old days. I was glad to see that it had not only survived, but had proved irrepressible by circumstance. Perhaps, I thought, it was my presence here that had brought it out—in which case, perhaps I would be able to do him good, to stop whatever rot seemed to have set in somewhere deep in the metaphorical roots of his soul.

Rowland sat down, and made himself comfortable. He looked at me, a trifle quizzically, while those thoughts ran through my mind. Then, very abruptly, he said: "How did Magdalen die, exactly?"

I had to pause to collect myself. "Poison, apparently," I said. "I can't say, *exactly*, because Rosalind wouldn't be any more specific than that, but she said that it's highly unlikely to have been an accident, and certainly wasn't murder."

"No," Rowland murmured. "Definitely not murder."

"You can't blame Rosalind," I told him. I felt a slight twinge of incongruity about the fact that I was defending her, even though the conversation we'd had in her car while circling Heathrow had probably had no other purpose than to persuade me to come to her defense, if necessary—but I really did mean it.

"I'm not," was Rowland's reply. I didn't believe him.

"She tried to help Magdalen," I told him. "She was genuinely distressed that she hadn't been able to. There's no way in the world that Rosalind could be held responsible for her death."

"Nobody's accusing her," Rowland said, his voice taking on a edge of resentment.

"Actually," I continued, perhaps recklessly, "she hinted that you might know more about the causes of Magadelen's death than she did. I assume you've been in communication with Magdalen, at least occasionally."

His pallor seemed to be intensifying further as I spoke, and the effort he was making to contain his emotion became visible. It was almost as if he, not I, had been the one traveling for more than a day, disorientated by a shift in time-zones. I still felt quite well. It had obviously been a bad idea to raise the subject of Magdalen's death so soon, and I felt guilty about making things worse with my own insensitivity. There was no way of deflecting him now, though.

"Very occasionally," he said, in response to my unwise prompt. "Poisoned? Was that the word Rosalind actually used?"

I nodded, not trusting myself to say anything.

"A trifle vague," he said, pensively. "Not like Rosalind, at all." He made a very visible effort, then, to collect himself, and altered his tone decisively to say: "I'm really not sure what she's trying to communicate, if anything. Lack of information sometimes speaks volumes, but...it really doesn't matter, does it? Dead is dead. Poor Mag. I suppose Rosalind blames me?"

"I honestly don't think so," I hastened to say. "When I spoke to her, she seemed to me to be blaming herself. I don't think it was an act."

Rowland raised his eyebrows slightly. "You don't know her" he said. "It's not her style to blame herself—but I might be wrong. I suppose we all come face to face with mirrors occasionally. She'd been feeding Mag drugs, of course—trying to 'cure' her misery and confusion?"

"She admitted that. Nothing chemically brutal, she insisted, and nothing experimental. Although she's reported to be heavily into olfactory psychotropics at present—the new aromatherapy, some of the newsfeeds call it—she says that she didn't try anything experimental on Magdalen. She told me that some of the stuff she gave her was just sugar pills—placebos—intended to have a purely psychosomatic attempt....but nothing worked."

Rowland's eyes weren't as blue as Rosalind's, but they were capable of appearing to flare up in a similar fashion. I had always been able to tolerate Rowland's gaze better than anyone else's, except Magdalen's, but not when he looked at me like that. I must have been blushing in confusion.

"That's what she told you?" he said, sharply.

It was all I could do to prevent myself stammering when I replied: "I believed her Rowland. I really do think it's true. I know that you and Rosalind have never seen eye to eye, but you can't doubt that she loved Magadalen. I can't believe that any treatment she attempted made matters any worse. She just wasn't able to make them any better. The reasons why she was blaming herself go much deeper—all the way back to your conception, I suspect."

"I doubt that," Rowland said, flatly. After a pause, though, he went on: "But you're right about her not being able to make things better." He paused again, still trying to collect himself, to recover the upbeat mood he had briefly attained while telling me about the fruit-trees and vegetables grafted on to the roots of his home. Finally, he deliberately adopted a lighter tone to say: "It wasn't anyone's fault. Poor Mag was unhappy because her circumstances were unhappy, not because of any chemical imbalance in the old tumor."

"Tumor?" I queried. It was so long that I'd heard the phrase used that it took me a moment or two to remember that, in Rowland's private parlance, the "old tumor" was the human brain. His notion of evolutionary theory wasn't entirely orthodox. He had always presented it as a joke, but I think he had been seriously committed to it, even while we were doing old Fliegmann's course together, attempting to plumb the still-mostly-hidden depths of practical neurology.

He smiled, albeit a little thinly, at my memory lapse. "We *have* let things slide haven't we?" he said. "I don't suppose you've got any more excuse than I have, because there isn't one—but we both know that it goes with the intellectual territory. And you're here now, aren't you? I've given you a bedroom just across the hallway from mine, near the sitting-room…just the way it used to be when we were sharing that house in Chiswick we rented when we were students."

I remembered that house very well. He, Magdalen and I had lived in it for five years, through most of our undergraduate and all of our postgraduate years. It had been extremely convenient, at the time, to have friends who had received their own independent legacies from Roderick the Great, even if I had perforce become something of a parasite on their generosity. The happiest times of my life had been spent in that house.

"I couldn't give you the lab next door to mine, though," Rowland added. "You're on a different floor, I'm afraid. I'll show you how to get there in a little while. It's very simple—the blue button in the elevator array."

"Which button gives access to your lab," I asked, automatically rather than curiously.

"Mine's a little out of the way," he said, not answering the question. "It requires all kinds of special facilities. I'll show you round the rest of the labyrinth, though, in the course of the next day or two. I think you'll be very interested in some of my experimental stocks. Roderick would have been proud of me—and, I hope, suitably amazed."

"I think Leon Gantz might have been amazed too," I said, "had he lived long enough to see this place. He'd be delighted with the way you've used the local silt as a matrix, and tickled pink by your adventures in plantation-grafting."

The nostalgic memories and feelings kept flooding back. When Rowland and I had taken our course in civil engineering we'd been partners in practical classes, and had prided ourselves on becoming rather adept—as we arrogantly thought—in the deployment of the standard bacteria used in modern cementation processes. The engineered bacteria, which could be adapted to almost any kind of raw materials, had already wrought their first revolution by then, and were helping to transform whole vast areas of land where it had been impossible to build in the past: deserts, steppes and bare mountains alike. While the ecological engineers were transforming the world's environments, Gantz-inspired structural engineers were building entire new cities for people whose ancestors had never known adequate shelter; thanks to Leon Gantz, there need be no more shanty-towns in the world that was rising phoenix-fashion from the ashes of the Crash, even if great palaces on the scale favored by Rosalind were still the prerogative of the rich.

Rowland and I had been fired with a similar sense of mission in those days, both determined to use the tools that our education provided to their very best purpose, and to play our part in the Utopian remaking of the world. We had shared a sense of imaginative vision and an ambition that many of our fellows lacked, or so it seemed to us, which had helped to bring us together in spite of our intrinsic social awkwardness. We had both became increasingly and deliriously interested in the techniques of genetic engineering we were being taught, including those involved in the manufacture of gantzian bacteria as well as the manipulation of plants and invertebrates, and our friendship had been firmly founded in the dream of imparting new powers to these living instruments, which would equip them to perform ever-more-astounding miracles.

My progress, inevitably had been far more modest than our shared daydreams allowed, and I had virtually given up on gantzing techniques in order to concentrate on plants and, ultimately, on algae. Evidently, Rowland had contrived to maintain a broader front in his endeavors and ambitions. Leon Gantz would, indeed, have been proud of him—and so was I.

"I can't take sole credit for the idea of the house," Rowland told me. "If it hadn't been for the discussions I had with you… well, let's just say, for now, that the contribution you made, if only by way of inspiration, wasn't trivial." He was being generous—and the generous impulse seemed to be doing him good. A little color had returned to his cheeks.

"You've obviously made significant headway with the great integration," I said, attempting to be generous in my turn, but having no need to exaggerate to do so. The inevitable horizon of our dream had be the ultimate union of gantzing with other kinds of genetic engineering: the production of buildings that would be living organisms in themselves. Pioneers in our fields had been experimenting even then with the incorporation of living systems into the inert walls of gantzed structures, but their utilitarian assumptions had stopped them once they produced mechanisms that could fulfill narrowly-specified aims. They had produced houses that could put down tap roots into the ground on which they stood, to secure their own water-supplies, and living systems for the disposal of human wastes had been in use for some time, but the present generation of architects hadn't taken the process of integration much further than that in the ten years since I'd obtained my doctorate, being as-yet-unready to follow the dream for the dream's own sake.

"Absolutely," Rowland confirmed. "I'll give you the whole story later, when we have a little more time."

I nodded my head, having become momentarily incapable of speech. Enclosed within Rowland Usher's self-designed, self-constructed and self-maintained house, all those old dreams of our student days had suddenly come flooding back into my mind—all the projects that had gripped our collaborative imaginations before we had even started our careers, but which I had left behind in the interim. Obviously, he had been truer to his imagination than I had been to mine. I felt ashamed—and momentarily, I felt a twinge of envy. How had I slipped so far back, I wondered, while Rowland had continued to go forward? We had, after all, both been in love with Magdalen. How could it be, I wondered, that I had been existentially crippled by my unrequited love, as Magdalen seemed to have been by hers, while Rowland…?

The shame suppressed the envy, though, and I shunted the train of thought into a dead-end siding—as I seemed to have been doing with so many trains of thought since going through the gates of Eden once again, to re-entangle myself with temptation.

CHAPTER NINE

Because it was still not long after midday, in terms of local time, Rowland insisted on giving me a guided tour of the house once we had rested briefly in the study and I had assured him that I was not significantly jet-lagged. As I began to explore the remarkable house that Rowland had built for himself, conducted by the architect in person, I couldn't help falling ever further into submission to our old flights of fancy, and the more I saw, the more cause I had to wonder about how much progress his genius had made while mine had been plodding.

The castles in the air that I had built my college days had been, without exception, edifices of considerable beauty and profound charm, perhaps not so very unlike Rosalind's Crystal Palaces, although designed for human occupation rather than the accommodation of flowers. Rowland's imagination had always had a greater originality and wildness about it, which some might have called surreal and others Gothic, although I always thought of it as simply Romantic, in spite of Rowland's distaste for that appellation.

No one could say that the strange masterpiece that Rowland had elevated from the silt of the great swamp bore any resemblance to a Crystal Palace, but it had an elegance of its own as well as an awesome complexity. Rowland had referred to its internal layout as a labyrinth, and so it seemed to be, but it was far more than any mere exercise in enigmatic convolution.

The internal walls seemed slightly less than solid, but not because they resembled a supercooled liquid. They had a superficial texture not unlike soft flesh, and gave the impression that they might be capable of a certain sluggish protoplasmic flow. I have to admit that this suggestion gave me an uneasy feeling when Rowland took me down into the regions beneath the "residential floor"—the "bowels," as I immediately began to think of them—and recalled to my mind the legend of Jonah who had been swallowed by a "great fish," or, as the writer presumably meant to imply, a whale.

Commencing the tour seemed to fill Rowland with a new enthusiasm, and I was thankful that the awkward conversation about Magdalen's death was now out of the way. He was obviously eager to show me the house, and to have someone whose opinion he valued to witness his triumphs. He guided me through the spiraling smooth-walled corridor that curved eccentrically around the internal "organs" of the house, its several branches giving it the appearance that it might extend for miles, and he showed me the principal lateral corridors that connected the spirals, like the chemical bonds in some crazy parody of the DNA double helix. All the corridors were softly lighted by artificial bioluminescence, which was slightly too ruddy and subdued for my taste, but not unsuited to their apparent fleshiness. They were not exactly cool, and the air was surprisingly humid, but the temperature was not too high to be uncomfortable, and I was only sweating moderately.

Perhaps it was only because of his enthusiasm, and a lack of practice in sustained conversation, that Rowland's voice began to stumble as he pointed out the features of his dwelling, occasionally stuttering over simple sentences. He gave the impression, however, of being slightly intoxicated—although I was certain that he had only drunk water down on the quay and up in the study. I felt obliged to suggest that he might be too tired to give me the extensive tour he had planned and promised, and reminded him that we had all the time in the world to complete it on another occasion.

"You really don't need to worry," he assured me. "As I told you, I might have been overdoing things slightly. You're right about the tour, of course—there's far too much to see in one excursion—but we do need to go a little further, so that you're familiar with the basic layout. It will do me good to walk and talk for a while—although I can't leave my work for very long, I fear, and I'll have to leave you to your own devices soon enough. It's as well that you know where things are as soon as possible, so that you can find your own way around."

A sudden suspicion occurred to me, and I couldn't help voicing it. "You've been taking something while you put in long stints of work, haven't you? Not your mother's products, I assume, but chemical stimulants of some kind? Aether, perhaps?"

"The demands of the work leave me little choice," he told me, unrepentantly. "Sometimes, I need a little assistance to keep going. Yes, I take Aether. There's no problem—I know my practical neurology, just as you do. The compound's safer than its predecessors, and much safer than the cocaine that made Venezuela what it was before the bottom fell out of the market. I'm careful."

He did know all there had been to know about practical neurology ten years before, thanks to Professor Fliegmann, and I had no doubt that he was keeping closer tabs on current developments in all the branches of psychotropics than I was, but I wasn't convinced that the Rowland Usher I knew was capable of being *careful*. "Nothing that interferes with your neurotransmitters can ever be entirely safe," I said.

"Don't be sanctimonious," he retorted. "You did Fliegmann's course too—you took part in the experiments we undertook in consequence, and it certainly wasn't always you who got the placebo."

"That was different," I said.

"Was it? Just normal student folly, to be put away with other childish things? You know that it was more serious than that."

Our psychotropic experiments had certainly seemed more serious, at the time; but it *had* been just normal student folly— perhaps not so very foolish, though, given that we had made every attempt to inform ourselves, academically, as to the risks associated with playing games with "the old tumor." I didn't make the point aloud, though: I just stared at Rowland with what must have been an anxious expression.

"Oh, don't look at me like that," Rowland said. "I just need to boost my energy occasionally, when fatigue makes work difficult. I haven't taken anything at all today, in honor of your arrival—perhaps that's where I went wrong. Yes, the old tumor's a little out of sorts at the moment—but I'm not suffering withdrawal symptoms any more than I'm under the influence. I haven't become any sort of addict while I've been living in the wilds. I'll be all right in a minute—*please* don't worry"

He seemed determined to fulfill his prophecy, and by the time the minute was up, he seemed to have succeeded.

"Let's go," he said, his voice becoming firmer again.

So we went on—to the storehouses where the equipment he had ordered for my laboratory had been placed. I was briefly distracted by the task of checking the crates. Once we had done that, and taken a swift glance into some of the other storage-bunkers, I was able to admire the network of bioelectrical generators that fueled the air-conditioning, the elevators and the communication system.

Having briefly inspected the generating apparatus and the water-purification and waste-disposal apparatus—although very little of the latter was actually visible—we returned to the elevator in order to go up to the white-button region, where my as-yet-unequipped laboratory space was located, along with a number of chambers that seemed, in essence, to be miniature and opaque equivalents of Rosalind's showcases. They were filled with glass compartments containing specimens of various sorts. There were a few flowering plants, but the great majority of the glass cages contained insects in various stages of their development.

Here, at least, Rowland was able to pause, and lean against one of the cabinets, while I wandered around on my own tour of inspection.

The mature insects weren't particularly exotic, for the most part; they included beetles, moths and a few flies, but no bees. Without exception, however, they were unusually large— sometimes very large. The larvae and pupae were even larger, suggesting that future adults might be larger still…if they could survive the final phase of metamorphosis.

"I see that your experiments with induced giantism have gone way beyond the size of the conventional larval borers used in construction," I remarked. "How are you coping with the traditional biomechanical difficulties and problems with oxygen distribution to the tissues?"

"The difficulties aren't as extreme as you might think," he said, dismissively, adapting his tone to his negligent pose. "When insects first evolved, more than a hundred million years ago, they soon produced forms much larger than the ones Mother Nature produces today. The gene for producing hemo-globin is still included in the genomes of many insect species, and so are relics of the old control genes that organized and facilitated its distribution and circulation within larger bodies. The insects we know from Mother Nature's recent work are all exoskeletal specialists, but there's no reason why insectile chitin can't be adapted to endoskeletal structures of various kinds, to facilitate mechanical organization. Organizing the control genes isn't easy, of course, even with vertebrate models for reference, because the metamorphic phase introduces an extra level of complexity—but that has advantages as well as creating diffi-culties. It's not the kind of genetic engineering that we learned at Imperial, but it's a linear extension of the work that Roderick did in later life—in a very different direction from the one in which Rosalind elected to develop his work. She was always more interested in the flowers than the pollinators…nor that I read any crude sexist lesson into that, of course."

I looked at him a trifle skeptically, for more than one reason. All I said, though, picking on the most innocuous factor in his speech was "You're trying to produce insects with backbones? Insects with hearts and veins? Why?"

"Why?" he echoed. "That's not a question you'd have asked

ten years ago, Peter. Because Mother Nature didn't, and maybe I can. To say that she, like Rosalind, was more interested in the flowers would be putting the cart before the horse—and I certainly wouldn't want to get tangled up in silly mythological metaphors about Father Sky and Mother Earth—but what insects actually became, in the course of that chapter of the evolutionary story, was very heavily influenced by the rapid parallel evolution of the angiosperms. If the insects hadn't found all those new niches opening up, and committed so many of their species to symbiotic dependency on plant sexuality, the big picture might have worked out very differently.

"Primitive insects had the potential to produce descendants with far more of the characteristics we associate with vertebrates—but the vertebrates had got there first, albeit hesitantly. Thanks to the legacy thy inherited from the fish in the sea they invaded the land with lots of evolutionary scope and momentum already in hand. The insects took the road of least resistance—which is the road that natural selection always takes. Clever genetic engineering allows us to go back in time now, in a manner of speaking, with a view to expanding the insects' early genetic potential in ways that natural selection never found profitable. Why? Just *because*. What other motive do I need? Giantism might be the most obvious aspect of it, but it's far from being the only one—there's much more. "

I cast my eye around the room we were in. "*Much* more," I repeated. "You mean, in other rooms than this?"

He did, but he also seemed to think that he had done enough, for the time being. "There's lots to talk about in that regard, when we have the time," he told me. "There are a lot of gleams in my paternal eye…but you're right that there's not much more to see in here but huge larvae, bloated beetles and pupae that aren't able to produce live imagoes. Sometimes, I get ahead of myself, seeing far more potential in my achievements than I've actually contrived to accomplish. You know how it is— you remember how it *was*, when we were students. Don't tell me that you aren't playing God-games with your algae, without ever bothering to ask yourself *why?*"

I did remember, and knew that I was guilty as charged, with respect to the algae—and I couldn't help feeling a slight thrill at the idea that, in entering the room, I'd stepped back in time, by ten years as well as a hundred million. This was, indeed, the kind of work we had dreamed of doing, back then—and if we had asked ourselves why, in those days, we would indeed have been perfectly satisfied to answer: *Just because*." Beating Mother Nature at her own game had always seemed reason enough.

"Yes," I confirmed, "I do know how it is, and I'm remembering more of how it *was* with every passing moment. I'm sure that we will have a lot to talk about, and not just about giant beetles and genuine dragonflies—although I doubt that my algae can compete in terms of glamour."

Rowland seemed pleased by this response, and he led me back into the corridors with the evident intention of moving on to the next phase of his conducted tour—but his enthusiasm, or at least his energy, seemed suddenly to weaken again. This time, he gave in.

"That's enough for now," he said. "It's almost dinner time anyway." He changed direction and led me to an elevator—not the same one that we had used before, although it had the same triangular array of buttons.

We went back up to the floor where the bedrooms and the study were located, where there was also a dining-room.

"Half an hour," he said, before disappearing into his bedroom.

I had plenty to do in the interim, and when I made my way back to the dining-room, once the thirty minutes had elapsed, I found the table set for four and Rowland already seated. Adam and Eve had evidently been busy preparing food, but had not anticipated that we would appear quite so soon; Rowland and I sat for a further fifteen minutes, conscientiously talking about nothing in particular, until the others joined us, bringing a tureen of soup with them.

The soup was anonymous, compounded out of vegetables

and fungi—and possibly algae too—that were no longer identifiable, but it wasn't unpleasant. It was followed by a fillet of some kind of fish, accompanied by small potatoes and assorted green vegetables; I didn't recognize the species of the fish, but the taste was better than tolerable.

"This is a special occasion," Rowland told me. "As I said before, the routine fare will be tissue-cultured meat—but the river fish are making a reasonably strong comeback in these parts. Adam's developing considerable skill with a spear, although it has to be said that the shallow pond around the house doesn't pose much of a challenge when the weather's calm. The fish are unwary—and likely to remain so for quite some time, given that Adam doesn't let very many of his targets get away."

Adam smiled at the compliment. "Weather good today," he observed. "Not tomorrow. Day after, big storm. So Met Office says."

For a moment, I thought he was making a joke, but then realized that satellite-based weather-forecasting could issue reports for sparsely-inhabited regions just as easily as heavily-populated ones. There might be no weather control hereabouts, for lack of sophisticated wind-farming apparatus, but the available newsfeeds could still issue predictions for the local area.

"Don't worry," Rowland, said, mistaking the reason for my momentary reflection. "The storms aren't excessively violent at this time of year, and the house can stand up to the most powerful hurricanes. Some day, I ought to install apparatus to steal the energy of the wind, but I haven't managed to find a gap in the schedule thus far."

The dessert proved to be some kind of chocolate confection, very sweet and glutinous. The coffee was served very strong, in tiny cups. It was good, but not the sort of coffee over which one could linger; two mouthfuls, and it was gone, administering a sudden caffeine hit to the bloodstream. Rowland certainly made no attempt to linger over his, getting up abruptly as soon as he'd gulped it down and offering profuse apologies for having to leave me alone.

"God-work is demanding," I conceded, graciously, refraining from raising the question of how he expected to work far into the night, given that he'd been exhausted by mid-afternoon, "especially for mere mortals. Will I see you later?"

"Not tonight," he replied, unsurprisingly. "If you need anything, phone Adam and Eve—their apartment's on the same corridor as our bedrooms. If you want to continue exploring, feel free—but be careful you don't get lost. Stick to the corridors I've shown you, until I have time to show you the rest."

I had no intention of trudging through any more corridors, though. In spite of the caffeine hit, I was conscious of being weary myself. It had been a long day—far longer than usual, in terms of daylight, given that the transatlantic flight had been traveling ahead of the sun, and my limbs were in need of rest. Indeed, when I thought about it, I suspected that it might have been wiser to give the coffee a miss, in order to catch up on my sleep without delay.

Rowland disappeared, after offering more apologies for not having been able to give me a more thorough introduction to the house. I found my own way back to my bedroom easily enough.

I spent a few minutes looking out of the window and admiring the dusky view. The harbor was on the northern face of the house, and my bedroom faced south, so I was looking out over the little patch of land that Rowland had called a "kitchen garden" and the still grey water of what looked from this vantage point more like a wide moat than a lagoon, toward the vast arc of mangroves on the far shore. Rowland's "plantations"—cultivated patches of varying size situated in what looked like natural clearings, by virtue of their irregular shapes and spacing—were clearly visible as a kind of patchwork, although it was impossible to make out exactly what was being grown in each one, given the distance and the twilight. Beyond that evidence of culture, however, there was nothing but a sea of green wilderness.

I knew that at least one branch of the river was in there somewhere, snaking southwards in a dozen or more substantial threads that would ultimately combine into a single powerful stream, but none of the major watercourses was distinctly visible from where I stood. In the rapidly-fading light, the regenerated forest was reminiscent of a single vast organism, within whose body the various braches of the Orinoco were flowing, as if through arteries and veins. Doubtless there would be flowers in there too—gorgeous tropical blooms of all shorts, including water-lilies more than a meter across—but there were none of those on the water surrounding the house, which looked quite still, although it had to be in complex motion, at least in the form of undercurrents. The river-water never ceased to ease its way toward the sea, even in its backwaters, and we were not quite beyond the reach of the tides. The quietness of the air and the low clouds was equally illusory; I was actually standing at the focal point of one of Mother Nature's most active regions, about as far away from domesticated England as could be.

For a moment, I regretted having left home—but only for a moment.

I went to bed, knowing that I wouldn't be able to sleep immediately, in spite of my physical fatigue, but quite prepared to lie awake and think, given that Rowland had given me far more food for thought than I'd carried with me on to the plane.

I could have taken up any number of cues or threads, of course, but one phrase that had stuck in my mind, although I hadn't reacted to it at the time, was "pseudo-symbiotic dependency on plant sexuality." In itself, it was just standard biojargon, but what made it significant, in Rowland's mouth, was its marked deviation from the jargon that Roderick and Rosalind had popularized, whose ideological foundation-stone was the notion of "dedicated symbiotic partnership."

In Roderick and Rosalind's world-view, the relationship between insects and flowering plants was authentic symbiosis, authentic partnership and—with all the implications that the word could carry—authentic dedication. Flowers made special provision to feed certain kinds of insects, having been designed by natural selection to do so because of the advantage gained from the transfers of pollen effected by those insects in the course of their feeding. There were, of course, countless other insect species, cousins of the obliging symbiotes, which took without providing any service in return—predators and parasites—but in the world-view of the Hive of Industry, they were a peripheral issue, mere passengers on an evolutionary bus driven and steered by the fundamental symbiotic relationship. There were other plants too, which relied on the wind to distribute their pollen, or simply did not bother, idly committing themselves to asexual reproduction or to incestuous self-pollination, but they too were sidelines and backwaters, far from the heart of the evolutionary narrative—at least in the world-view of the Hive.

During the days of the bee problem, of course, the world-view of the Hive had seemed patently obvious. There had been a moment—a moment that had stretched over decades—when it looked as if the loss of the pollinators responsible for maintaining the greater part of humankind's crop-species might precipitate an abrupt worldwide food shortage. Even Roderick the Great had not been able to prevent some temporary shortages, but he and those working in his shadow had succeeded in smoothing out the decline as well as facilitating the recovery. He had negotiated and guided the transition—and he had done it within the framework of the crucial symbiotic relationship, the crucial partnership, and the age-old dedication.

But Rowland, it seemed, saw things differently. He saw a "pseudo-symbiotic dependency" in which the insects were exploited by "plant sexuality"—fed, as even slaves were fed, but not accepted into genuine partnership.

The concept of symbiosis does not, of course, imply equality of effort or endeavor; like any kind of trade, it's a matter of exchanging a good that one party needs or desires for a different good that the other party needs or desires. In any kind of trade, there is scope for exploitation, and it's arguable that no trade is every truly free or fair, no matter what Utopian gleams may shine in the eyes of purist economists. In every commercial deal, cynics will readily tell you, one of the two parties is getting screwed. There's no earthly reason to think that things work differently in the bosom of Mother Nature.

On the other hand, it isn't always obvious which party to the deal is the one getting screwed, and the wheels of trade would spin a lot less smoothly if it weren't for the fact that, in many deals, both parties can at least delude themselves into thinking that they're coming out ahead.

One might think, on first glancing at the bee/flower relationship, that it's the bees who are getting the better part of the deal. They, after all, are the ones getting fed; all the flowers are getting out of it is sex—and orgasm-less sex at that. In the hierarchy of needs, eating comes way ahead of....well, we shouldn't call it "screwing," having already compromised that item of metaphorical jargon within the argumentative frame, so let's call it "love." On the other hand, as even folk wisdom has observed, it's the bees who are doing all the physical work, always busy, endlessly toiling away. And it would not be irrelevant to observe, at this point, that the worker bees who are doing the toiling appear not only to be doing it on behalf of the flowers, but also on behalf of their own queens. Worker bees get fed, but they get no love. Only queens, as seemingly idle as flowers, save for one nuptial flight per annum, produce offspring—and although the equally idle drones get to have sex as well, it's difficult to think of them as "screwers" in the economic sense, when only one drone per annum gets to do it, once and once alone, and dies immediately afterwards.

There is, of course a sociobiological logic to the hive society of bees. Because bee males are chromosomally X while bee females are XX, each female bee shares three-quarters of her genetic component with her sisters, and only fifty per cent with her mother or daughters. It therefore makes sense, from a gene's point of view, to situate itself inside a female organism that invests her effort in the multiplication of sisters rather than daughters. Viewed from that angle, a queen bee isn't really an autocratic monarch at all, but a mere instrument, operated by the workers to produce more workers—ditto for the drones. The genes stuck in the queen and the favored drone do, of course, have the evolutionary compensation of producing lots of offspring, but the fact remains that sisters are worth more, in the brutal currency of the genetic economy of bees, than other kin.

In that world-view, therefore, the worker bees aren't really toiling on behalf of their queens, but on behalf of their own Machiavellian genes—and their relationship with the flowers can be construed in the same way.

Thanks to the symbiotic exchange, the flowers get to produce more copies of their own genes, by virtue of the exchange of pollen, while the workers bees get the fuel that enables the to produce more sisters. Put that way, it look like a more equal exchange, a fairer trade--in which context it makes sense to speak in terms of "dedicated symbiotic partnerships," much as dewy-eyed economists speak of "free trade."

Roderick, on the other hand, saw it as "pseudo-symbiotic dependency." Roderick thought that the apparent equality was an illusion, but that it was the bees, not the flowers, that were the ones getting screwed. Why?

Well, given that we live in a world in which ten billion people have effectively starved to death within the last hundred years, it's very easy to be acutely aware of the importance of eating, and it seems perfectly obvious that food is more important than sex, from the viewpoint of individual survival. Evolution, however, isn't very much concerned with individual survival. Evolution is all about speciation, and the cost of speciation is the routine death of millions or billions of individuals.

Dying is only one aspect of natural selection, but without death, evolution would be exceedingly slow. Death speeds things up dramatically; death is what clears out the old to make way for the new. The life of the whole ecosphere thrives on the not-quite-random deaths of individuals. From the viewpoint of evolutionary success, starvation is not an evil but a good; from the viewpoint of evolutionary success, organisms that feed other organisms—and there's no choice in the elementary fact, because every organism is inevitably prey to predators and host to parasites—do well to feed selectively, to offer their bounty to organisms that are useful to them.

The destiny of plants, fundamentally, is to be eaten; that's the logic of the situation. Cleverness, in plants, is not only invested in slowing down the process of being eaten, but also in directing and orchestrating the eating process, in the interests of the other aspect of natural selection, which is reproduction. Natural selection works, not merely because the less effective organisms die, but because the more effective ones reproduce. In the world-view of evolution, individual reproduction is just as vital as individual death. In evolutionary terms, starvation is good, and so is sex. In the context of evolution, the plant that trades its own organic substance for pollination—or the distribution of seeds—is a making a good deal, at a bargain price.

That might seem odd, given that individual plants—unlike most animals—don't actually need sex at all to reproduce. They can do it vegetatively. Primitive organisms do it all the time. Individual bacteria and algae routinely go through life reproducing asexually. But asexual reproduction, like not dying, doesn't facilitate evolution. From the viewpoint of the entire ecosphere, asexual reproduction is stagnation; what natural selection favors is genetic exchange, genetic recombination and genetic experimentation. Natural selection always favors sex.

Mother Nature loves love and death alike, as if they were siblings—non-identical twins, different in kind but equal in value. In the hierarchy of evolutionary needs, as opposed to the hierarchy of individual needs, food is cheap and sex is priceless.

From the viewpoint of evolutionary success rather than individual success, therefore—which is to say, from the viewpoint of enduring for hundreds of millions of years rather than one or a few—when the angiosperms and the insects were mounting their parallel conquest of the land, the flowers that entered into close association with specialist pollinators were the ones doing the screwing, and the insects drawn into that dependency were the ones getting screwed.

So, at least, Rowland Usher saw the situation, if his jargon could be trusted.

Perhaps, I thought, it wasn't entirely surprising that Rowland saw the situation differently from his mother and his sisters—but there was nothing simple or straightforward about that situation, literally or metaphorically. Rosalind wasn't really a Queen Bee and Magdalen had never been a shrinking violet. Evolution might be progressive, and it certainly had a beauty about it, but it was irredeemably, horribly messy. Order and grandeur eventually emerged out of the chaos, but they were direly hard-won.

Thus far, genetic engineering, in spite of all its fabulous triumphs—like selective breeding before it—had only made marginal improvements on the fundamental messiness of natural selection. We were still novices at the God-game, having made a fairly conspicuous dent in the economics of death, at the levels of our own individuality and the unnatural selection of other species, but not yet having mastered the economics of sex, even in terms of the design of new species, let alone at the level of our own individuality.

In purely physical terms, of course, we now had sufficient control over our own reproduction to permit men like Peter Bell the First to revert to the stagnancy of asexual reproduction, and women like Rosalind Usher to pick and choose the sperm that would fertilize her eggs in order to produce daughters by the score—and sons too, had she wished—but physical terms were not the whole of the problem, and mere versatility in physical terms could not be counted as its solution.

At that point in my train of thought, not unnaturally, the personal took over from the intellectual—always a danger when one is tired, especially if one actually goes to sleep and dream-logic takes up the reins of argument. Fortunately, I rarely retain more than the vaguest fleeing memory of my dreams when I awake again, and although I'm sure that my reflections on the evolution of insects and flowers and their complex economic transactions produced some nightmarish imagery, once they metamorphosed into dreams and lost the control of rationality,

I retained no clear picture of that imagery once reason resumed its empire.

Did I see Magdalen, Rosalind and Rowland in those dreams? Very probably. Did I see monstrous giant insects of various kinds? Almost certainly. Did I see flowers magnified in their gorgeousness and sexuality? Quite possibly. Did I see myself? Surely not. Even when I am manifestly present in my own dreams—and I often do not seem to be "there" are at all—I never *see* myself. There are no mirrors in my dreams. I have no idea how rare or common that might be.

At any rate, I cannot report on the remainder of the journey traveled by that particular train of thought, if it did continue after I fell asleep, because I cannot remember where it went. Like Rosalind's olfactory psychotropics, its effects, if any, were beyond the reach of consciousness.

Does it matter? At the time, I thought not—but as you will doubtless have realized by now, much of what I thought at the time eventually turned out to be misguided. Perhaps, if I had remembered my dreams as well as my stubbornly rational, seemingly-scientific chains of logic, I would have realized sooner what actually lay behind Magdalen Usher's untimely death.

It wouldn't have made any difference, though. There was nothing I could have done, no matter how much I had realized, any more than there had been anything Rosalind could do, or Rowland, or Magdalen herself. It was a Romantic tragedy, inescapable and unstoppable, at least by our science.

At least Rosalind and Rowland tried—and if people like us do not try, what hope is there that anyone will ever succeed?

CHAPTER TEN

When I did wake up, I lay silently in my bed for some time. I had closed the shutters over the window before going to bed, simply by turning a switch that had caused them to come together like eyelids, so the room was dark—but not entirely dark, for there was a slight residual bioluminescence in the walls: a sort of integral night-light. When I opened my eyes, unhurriedly, I continued to lie still. I thought that I could perceive a vibration in the dull, warm walls. I wondered briefly whether it might be the echo of something external, like heavy rain. I was in the tropics, after all, and although the storm promised by Adam's equivalent of the Met Office wasn't due until the following day, it might well be raining. I decided, however, that the faint sensation was more likely to be due to some mysterious internal process at work within the living fabric of the fabulous structure. After a time, I found it strangely comforting, as if it were a subliminal lullaby, but I resisted the temptation to drift back into peaceful sleep. There was work to be done, and I was anticipating a long and busy day.

I made my way to the dining-room without making any advance inquiry or notifying anyone of my intention, but I found Rowland there, and we breakfasted together. He seemed less pale than he had the day before, in spite of the fact that he must have worked long into the night; if his condition the day before had been an effect of abandoning the use of some psychotropic substance with which he had been experimenting, he had now overcome the slight withdrawal symptoms—one way or another. He told me, however, that he didn't have time to continue the guided tour of the house that he had begun the previous afternoon.

"My own work still requires my presence," he explained, "but you'll want to set up your own lab anyhow. Adam will help you, but without a knowledgeable assistant of your own you'll find that it's a slow process—he's willing, but not expert."

"There's no rush," I said. "I won't be able to start collecting specimens until the day after tomorrow at the earliest, if there's going to be a storm, and for at least a fortnight, I won't be doing anything but observing and sorting. All I'll need, for quite some time, is an abundant supply of tanks and microscopic apparatus. I'll set up the sequencers and the vector cultures, of course, but I doubt that I'll being dong any genomic analysis for a week or the days, let alone any tinkering."

"I have some efficient vectors for use in plants," Rowland told me. "Some of them might be effective in algal cells, or easily adaptable to that purpose. I'll bring you some samples when I have time."

He didn't bring them that day, which I spent organizing my laboratory in a careful and painstaking fashion. Adam was with me all the time, and proved to be more helpful than Rowland had led me to expect. Not only was the Venezuelan quick on the uptake in realizing what we were aiming to do, but he was curious about the equipment. I was surprised by his apparent unfamiliarity with instruments of which Rowland must make routine use, but I quickly realized that he had never been in Rowland's laboratory.

I had hoped to seek some enlightenment from Adam as to what ultimate aim Rowland might have in mind in experimenting with insect giantism, but soon concluded that he would not be able to tell me anything useful. Indeed, the boot was soon switched to the other foot, as Adam sought enlightenment from me, not only about what Rowland might be doing, but what I proposed to do.

I tried to explain, but it was hard work; Rowland had not

bothered to provide him with the most elementary education in genetics—indeed, had probably deliberately refrained from so doing—and although Adam's English was perfectly viable for everyday communication, he simply did not have the vocabulary to cope with biological science. It took me several hours to explain to him where algae fit into Mother Nature's scheme of things, and why they were significantly different from plants, properly speaking. Almost as soon as I had my microscope set up he wanted to look through it, to see for himself why algal cells were not like plant-cells. He seemed fascinated by the fine structure of cells, but he had some way to go before he would be able to comprehend the mysteries of DNA.

He seemed disappointed that neither Rowland or I seemed to be interested in fish, which he regarded as a significant potential resource, but he seemed to approve of the fact that I was at least interested in species that provided fodder for fish. He didn't understand why anyone should be interested in insects, except to kill those that bit or stung, and the prospect of breeding giants of the kind lay far beyond the limits of his notion of sanity. Nevertheless, Adam evidently had an enormous respect for Rowland and was obviously very conscious of owing him a huge debt of gratitude. He and Eve could probably have contrived to make a living in their homeland without his patronage, but they would have had to take up residence in a city or labor on a plantation of a very different kind from Rowland's flamboyant grafting enterprise. Eventually, I began to understand what Rowland had meant when he said that Adam and Eve weren't entirely sure whether they were living in Heaven or Hell, although it might have been more apt to say that they did not know whether they were living in a palace in God's Eden or the Devil's.

Either way, Adam seemed content, and I imagined that Eve was too. They didn't seem to have experienced any temptation that might have prompted them to leave, or led to their expulsion.

I tried, as best I could, to enhance Rowland's seemingly

divine attributes and dismiss the apparently diabolical ones out of hand. I told Adam about Roderick, and how his work on specialist pollinators had complemented the wholesale development of new primary producers to feed renascent humankind. Such was the ineptitude of my oversimplified explanations, however, that I suspect that the poor fellow took away the inference that Rowland was trying to produce bigger insects in order to service bigger flowers, and thus produce bigger fruits and seeds. I had to be content to let him think that I was trying to manipulate algae merely in order to produce better food for fish and to obliterate toxic algal blooms—of which he had some experience.

By the time we finished work for the day and went to meet Rowland for dinner, I had almost begun to wonder whether Adam might be right, and had begun to ask myself why I wasn't directing my efforts as an engineer toward the production of more useful crop-species, and species that might enhance the eventual revival of the marine ecosystems whose injuries we had not yet been able to assess in full. The world in which I was living was, however, replete with pedestrian kelp-men and would-be fish farmers, and there seemed to be room enough in it for researchers interested in more fundamental and more esoteric questions.

The main course at dinner was, as promised, centered on a joint of tissue-cultured beef, but it hadn't been cultured in the house. It had come from the freezer, having been imported from Brazil.

Roderick apologized yet again for not having had time during the day to show me more of the wonders of his residence, and told me that he was now too tired to begin repairing the omission that evening. He seemed slightly triumphant in reporting his tiredness, as if it somehow proved that my anxieties of the previous day regarding the use of stimulants had been misplaced.

He offered, instead of continuing the tour, to spend the evening with me in comfortable relaxation, and to make good on the promise he'd made earlier by filling in some of the detail of the researches that had led to the construction of the edifice—which, he claimed, would form an important component of his intellectual legacy, when he got around to publishing an account of them.

Naturally, I agreed. The two of us settled down in the study after coffee, with a decanter of some sort of home-made wine. It wasn't the produce of the legendary "noble grape," but it had a perfectly tolerable taste.

Outside, the evening was becoming calm again, after a blustery day, and the sky was bright blue, gradually darkening as the sun set—but Rowland told me that it was definitely the proverbial calm before the storm, and that the situation would change dramatically overnight. "We'll be snug here, though," he assured me.

"As bugs in a rug?" I suggested—but couldn't raise a smile from the insect man.

"You doubtless recall from discussions we had more than a decade ago," he said, switching into a conscientiously earnest mode, "that I was always impatient with the traditional gantzing techniques that were in common use in our youth, which we were expected to learn in a more-or-less slavish fashion in the course we took in civil engineering."

"I do," I confirmed, with a wry smile.

"One of my chief interests then—which we shared, as you've already remarked—was the necessity of integrating better artificial living systems into the structure of buildings. Although biotechnologists had already developed methods of artificial photosynthesis, they had few advantages over natural systems, and I knew that truly sophisticated living dwellings wouldn't come into being until artificial photosynthesis had been considerably improved, which might well require thirty of fifty years. It seemed to me that the problem was better approached in the meantime by modifying living material for structural purposes rather than trying to add artificial life to structures formed by gantzing cementation. Roderick had already begun adapting architectural bacteria to work with supercooled liquids, but that seemed a very limited field."

"Rosalind's done some good work along those lines," I put in. "Have you seen pictures of the marquee she designed for the funeral?"

"Yes I have," he said, curtly, "but as I say, that's not really relevant to what I've done. I started off trying to work with woody structures, perhaps under Professor Crowthorne's influence, but I soon figured out that I needed to retreat further down the evolutionary tree."

"To fungi?" I asked, knowing already that he didn't mean algae.

"Fundamentally, yes—but that entire subphylum suffers some crucial and awkward limitations. I figured that fungal chitin might be a useful basic matrix, but I knew that photosynthetic systems would have to be integrated into it at some stage, and figured that it would also be profitable to import some animal systems too."

"Hybridization of plant and animal tissue is hellishly difficult," I observed. "Many have tried, but few have succeeded."

"I didn't even try," Rowland admitted. "Hybridization didn't seem to be the way to go. Not surprisingly, I figured that there might be a lot more scope in symbiosis. Rather than trying to design an edifice that was akin to a gigantic organism, it seemed to me that it might be better to devise one that was akin to a colony: a colony combining fungal and cnidarian flesh with molluskan and insect flesh, to combine the benefits of animal and fungal chitin with those of shell and coral."

I was genuinely impressed. "Chimerization rather than hybridization," I said. "There's a lot of interesting work going on in that line back home—but nothing as ambitious as the kind of hectic mix you're talking about. Have you really brought that off?" I looked around at the walls of the room with new respect, not having suspected them of so much internal complexity, at the protoplasmic level.

"This part of the house is relatively simple," he told me,

following the direction of my gaze. It isn't until you get down into the guts that the full extent of the…well, I suppose *chimerization* is as good a word as any…becomes obvious. What you're looking at now is mostly just gantz-enhanced chitin."

I suddenly formed a mental picture of the buttons in the elevator, and realized the significance of the four black buttons at the base of the isosceles triangle.

"You mean that the edifice extends downwards as well as upwards?" I said. "It has an elaborate network of cellars?"

"I suppose that *cellars*," he said, rather disdainfully, "is as good a word as any." He was deliberately repeating the formula he'd used only a few moments before, but his tone implied that the descriptive capability of the word was distinctly lacking this time. He didn't suggest any alternative, though. He'd already used "labyrinth" with respect to the parts of the house I'd seen, and presumably didn't fee that "bowels" was any more appropriate than "cellars." He'd already shown me the waterworks and sewerage, so the depths he was talking about now were deeper than that.

"As we discussed back in the old days," Rowland went on, "houses will one day be living hybrids of all kinds of flesh, harvesting the energy of the sun as plants do, moving as animals do, and providing every internal facility that biology can offer— but that's a long way in the future. My house simulates a more primitive kind of organism: a lowly saprophyte and scavenger, which draws its energy from the organic detritus of the silt out of which its walls are constructed.

"She's no more sophisticated, in terms of her nutrition, than many sedentary creatures which live in shallow seas, filtering food from the murky waters which overflow them. Her closest analogues, if you wish to think in such terms, are polyps, barnacles and tubeworms. She's alive and growing, though, with a great deal to scope for further development. Her saprophytic activity provides energy for numerous internal processes relying on what you call chimerization, although it really is more akin to symbiosis, in that many—though not all—of her subsidiary elements are disconnected from the basic biomass, resembling free-living organisms rather than the kind of grafts represented by the plantations.

"The Orinoco feeds the house's appetites very well, with all manner of decayed vegetable matter washed out of Venezuela's heartland. It serves as a veritable cornucopia to the network of filters that extend from her foundations."

"It's an impressive scheme," I readily conceded. "I look forward to seeing more of the detail in action."

A slight shadow passed over his expression—but whatever thought was behind it wasn't one he wanted to voice at present.

"You'll doubtless remember another of my fascinations," he continued, "which is similarly embodied in the architecture of the house. Ordinary gantzing processes use inert moulds—the cementing organisms simply bind the material brought to them, and the architect controls the shape of what they produce by crude mechanical means. Roderick's glass-workers are more creative than that, in terms of producing geometrical forms, but you'll remember my saying, back in our student days, that the real models for emulation were the nests of wasps and termites, or bower-birds and ovenbirds, the supporting structures of corals, and the astonishing forms of flowering plants and trees....in brief, the most sophisticated produce of control genes. Adapting control genes to function in any kind of hybrid is difficult, let alone a chimera or a colony—but it's not impossible. Again, my work in that respect is in its infancy, but I'm making progress. The structural elements of the house that are analogous to the xylem of a tree, the shell of a mollusk, the exoskeleton of an insect or the skeleton of a vertebrate, are all alive and active, subject to modification by the action of control genes. As you saw from the boat as you approached, she's hardly an architectural masterpiece—but she has potential. The mission is hardly started, let alone complete, but one day...."

He left that sentence incomplete.

"One day," I decided to finish for him, "the house will undergo a sort metamorphosis. At present, it's not unlike a sort of pupa…but it has the potential to shed its husk and reveal something much more spectacular."

He nodded, in apparent satisfaction. "I can't expect too much of this particular individual," he hastened to add, "but even if she can't live forever, or can't develop beyond a certain point, what we can learn from her will make an enormous difference to her offspring."

"You really do mean *her*, don't you?" I finally queried. I'd let the pronoun pass the first few times he's used it, assuming that it was a mere figure of speech, but now I wondered whether he really was attributing a sex to the house.

"The edifice incorporates individuals of many species and both sexes," he replied, "but we don't have a pronoun for a multiplex androgyne. Given that the house is intended to be the found an entire evolutionary sequence, though, I can't help but think of her as a mother as well as a rough draft."

"But you don't actually call her Rosalind the Second?" I remarked—too flippantly by half.

This time, he scowled. "Don't," he said, briefly. "Sore point."

I apologized.

"So," I said, hastily recapitulating, "the whole chimera—or colony—although it contains various aspects, and perhaps entire organisms, from the fungal, plant and animal realms, is modeled on a giant insect? A giant much vaster and infinitely stranger than the ones you showed me yesterday, but not dissimilar in kind. It has a metamorphic capacity built into it…albeit one that isn't likely to become manifest for a long time."

"It's too simple-minded to compare her pupal status to that of an insect," he said, reflectively rather than correctively. "Her primary builders are micro-organisms of various sorts, which associate and collaborate, more like the individual cells in a slime-mold or a Portuguese Man o'War than the various castes of a beehive. There's a sense in which the more complex organisms in the colony—the symbiotes of the elementary cells—are a supplementary presence, but I'm trying to make them more integral in terms of their reproductive cycles. They can't reproduce independently; they have to be born from the fundamental structure—but there are flaws in that process that I haven't worked out yet. Until I do, the possibility of reproducing the whole colony—mothering another House of Usher—remains out of reach."

"So you are prepared to call it the House of Usher, in spite of the Poesque precedent?" I suggested, trying not to sound flippant.

"You're prepared to answer to Peter Bell the Third, in spite of an even less prepossessing precedent," he reminded me. "You're prepared to struggle against the coincidental precedent rather than avoiding it. So am I. In time, my House of Usher will probably decay, and dissolve in the waters of the river….but not while I can sustain her, and not before she's at least helped to provide a plan for her successor, if not actually to spawn a living heir. I'm doing everything humanly possible to differentiate my House of Usher from Poe's. How are *you* doing?" He tried to sound sympathetically concerned, but couldn't quite manage it.

"In my work with algae?" I queried, deliberately misunderstanding him. He had, of course, been challenging me to demonstrate the extent of my own differentiation from Shelley's unfortunate Peter Bell the Third.

He smiled, and nodded his head, accepting the implicit rebuke. "With your algae, of course. Have you found anything that might be useful to my endeavors with the house?"

"Actually," I said, "there might be. You'd have to explain the genetics of your house in a great deal more detail before I can make practical suggestions, but if you were to look at what you're doing in terms of chimerization rather than symbiotic colony-formation…well, it turns out that algae can perform some weird tricks when the going gets tough, as it did during the Crash. You might think that the marine algae had a fairly easy ride, by comparison with land-based plants, but they had to cope with changes in salinity and temperature as well as radically disrupted ecosystems. They had a hard time."

"Go on," he prompted, seeming interested now—although it

was optimistic of me to assume that the challenge he'd offered a few moments earlier had been abandoned. Knowing Rowland as I did, I should have known that he wouldn't let it go.

"Algae are no strangers to chimerization," I said. "Lichens are a chimerical compound of fungi and single-celled algae, and there were numerous algal species that had taken up habitual residence in or on various plant and animal species in the pre-Crash ecosphere. It was only to be expected that more instances would show up, as evolution in the shifting littoral zones was forced into ultra-rapid mode, but the natural expectation would be that most of the algal species finding new niches of that sort would be single-celled green algae or simple strands of similar cells. I have found instances of that sort, but I've also found more complex associations, which require a certain amount of genetic collaboration: not quite chromosomal fusion—not yet, at least—but certainly chromosomal cross-functionality, control genes from both sets collaborating in the formation of compound individuals.

"The ones that are easiest to spot are, of course, the monsters—but they're mostly evolutionary rejects, scheduled for elimination by natural selection. The successes are less obtrusive—but examples are multiplying, and they include some surprising associations. I don't know what I'll be able to dredge up hereabouts, but what you've told me about your house suggests that it might be serving as a vital stimulus, spreading side-effects in all directions. I'm looking forward to finding out. None of that will surprise you, of course, given your theories about the contribution made by past genetic predation to the broad pattern of Earthly evolution. I presume that you haven't had second thoughts about that, as you're still referring to the human brain as the *old tumor*."

He raised his wine-glass to acknowledge the point.

Even orthodox evolutionists concede that viruses might have made a significant positive contribution to the evolution of more complex organisms, by incorporating extra genetic material into chromosomal complements, which offered raw material for natural selection, but Rowland had always wanted to broaden that notion out. Just as the harm that viruses did to individuals had to be balanced out against potential benefits in speciation—thus ensuring that natural selection would never eliminate them from the scheme of things—he thought that the deleterious effects of cancers and other growths within the body had to be balanced out, in the accountancy of natural selection, against the occasional potential benefit that the additional tissue-growth might provide.

In Rowland's view, the human brain was the product of tumorous growths, only one in a thousand of which might have proved harmless, and only one in a million immediately useful, but those rare instances being enough for natural selection to work with spectacular effect. Indeed, according to Rowland, every aspect of complex multicellular bodies had probably begun existence as a tumor. In his view, cancer deserved at least as much credit for evolutionary progress as point mutations in the genome whose effects did not include producing cancers.

"In that case," I said, taking his gesture as assent, "you'll doubtless be unsurprised to find Mother Nature attempting to duplicate, in her own slow and makeshift fashions, the same sort of innovations that you're trying to hasten along in your house-building."

He nodded his head. "You're right," he said. "If I'd thought about it in those terms, I would have expected it, and might even have gone looking for it—but as you say, Nature tends to be slow and unsteady. I'm trying to sprint, faster than even Roderick contrived to go. It might not come off, but...."

"Man's reach must exceed his grasp," I quoted, "or what's a Heaven for?"

"You really ought to ease up on the poetry, Peter," he advised me, probably meaning well. "Too much quotation channels thought and inhibits innovation."

I resisted the temptation to recite "The Haunted Palace" in full, although our situation surely warranted it.

"Trains of thought need tracks to run on," I told him.

"Only if their destination is fixed," he retorted. "We're supposed to be explorers, not commuters. We're supposed to be pioneers of trackless wilderness—trackless in every sense of the word. Your fondness for quotation is holding you back, Peter, weighing you down." The challenge was back again, sooner than I had anticipated.

"I'm a quotation myself," I murmured. "I can't help being a copy of a copy, blurred but still a victim of predestination. No matter how hard I try to be an innovation—and there's quite a distance between solid-state physics and the genetics of chimerization—I'll never entirely escape the railway system of my nature."

"You mustn't believe that, Peter," he told me earnestly. "Even if it were true, you shouldn't believe it—but it isn't true. You and I are geneticists, and we know the limits of genetic determinism. There's always scope for viruses and tumors, and lesser afflictions of a similar kind, as well as the power of the imagination—and I'm talking about the biological imagination, the *practical* imagination, not Romantic whimsy. You're not really Peter Bell the Third—you're Peter Bell the New. You need to move on. I have."

"Really?" I said, I trifle resentfully. "Have you moved on in *every* respect?"

When he'd told me that I needed to move on, he'd had Magdalen in mind, so he understood my response. We were friends; we understood one another—even after the long lapse of time during which we hadn't seen one another. So I believed, at any rate.

"Some things are easier to get past than others," he said, soberly and wisely, "but we have to try—one way or another."

CHAPTER ELEVEN

The following day, Rowland left me to my own devices again while he retreated to his mysterious underground laboratories to see to the progress of his mysterious experiments. I had plenty of work that I could be doing in my own lab, even in the absence of any research material, but to begin with, I watched the storm for a while through the windows of my room. I'd seen plenty of storms in England, of course, but this was my first opportunity to observe a tropical storm—not quite a hurricane, but certainly violent enough to be impressive. The pouring rain limited visibility, but I was able to study the ingenious ways in which the trees on the nearby shore yielded to the wind, preserving their foliage and branches as best they could against the assaults of the air.

As Rowland had promised, the house resisted the wind too, assisted by its curvature, which seemed able to deflect the airflow smoothly in spite of all its protuberances. It did not shake at all, nor did it produce the kinds of noises that English houses invariably did in English storms. It did not creak or groan, and the shutters on its windows did not rattle or bang. It was, in fact, eerily silent within the house, whose insulating walls and windows muffled the sounds generated outside: the splashing of the water, the whistling of the wind and the intermittent rumbling of thunder. The distant spikes of lightning seemed oddly perfunctory, though. I wondered, idly, how much damage a direct strike on the house might do, but the prospect did not seem unduly scary. I had no doubt that Rowland would have taken precautions against such an eventuality, for the house's sake as well as his own.

In ancient fiction, I knew, weather had routinely been used to reflect the emotional states of characters and the dramatic pitch of plots, but Rowland's House of Usher seemed to deny and defy that possibility. An observer within it, like me, was cocooned from all the effects of the storm's external urgency and fury. I was perfectly calm, in spite of the fact that I was watching a tropical storm. I was warm and dry, and the air I was breathing was still and pure. Emotion seemed almost impossible, at least as a reflection of that kind of external effect—and there did not seem to be any kind of well-defined plot in my presence, whose drama might be subject to acceleration and climax. All in all, watching the storm from my room was more like watching TV than actually participating in the life of the tropics.

When I left the room I intended to make my way to the lab, but I was in no particular hurry, and felt that I ought to look around a little, in order to become more familiar with the tunnels and lacunae formed by the natural honeycombing of the upper part of the house. Now that Rowland had explained a little more about the anatomy of the house and the way its construction had been undertaken, I realized that there was a fundamental natural pattern to the layout of the corridors and chambers, but the precise design of the rooms—not to mention the various connecting conduits that carried water, electricity and optical fibers—had obviously required supplementary work.

Supplementary work, in the ordinary gantzed structures with which I had long been familiar in England, is routinely carried out by drills and other steel tools, in association with de-cementing bacteria whose activity is precisely the opposite of the cementers, but that was not the case here. Rowland appeared to be using worms do to do his drilling and shaping, akin to the engineered organisms used to pulverize rocks like granite and basalt but more refined. Most such organisms, of course aren't really worms in the usually biological meaning; they're modified insect larvae, analogous to the beetle larvae popularly know as "woodworm." The common industrial types were equipped with jaws and rasps powerful enough to cope with stone and metal, but rarely had any sculptural ability beyond the facility to bore holes; Rowland's seemed to be more artistic—or, at least, a good deal cleverer.

With that sort of observation to be made, I spent far more time on the day of the storm studying the finer points of the house than setting up my own lab in readiness to receive specimens. I got lost several times, but only had to call on Adam's help once in returning to known spaces; on the other occasions, simple trial and error eventually sufficed. I didn't use the elevators at all, preferring to build a mental picture of the organization of the staircases. By mid-afternoon, I thought I had a good grasp of the upper floors—but I hadn't even found any stairways leading down to the "cellars" that presumably lay beneath the ground-floor warehouses and store-rooms, where Roland's laboratories were presumably located. I assumed that there had to be other means of access than the two central elevators, but I couldn't locate them, either because they were deliberately hidden or because my mental picture of the upper part of labyrinth was incomplete, blind to some crucial lacuna.

I did spend a little time in my lab, eventually, but I couldn't settle to any kind of productive work there and went back up to the living-quarters to consult Adam about the likelihood that we would be able to go out the following day.

The indigene shook his head sorrowfully. "Storm dying, but not dead," he told me. "Wind and rain—not good for boat. Best wait one more day."

That didn't seem unduly inconvenient; I wasn't experiencing any impatience. I was looking forward to resuming my evening discussions with Rowland, but I didn't feel any particular urgency about that, either. When he and I retired to the study after dinner, though, I asked him about the refinements he had made to the boring larvae.

"Insect larvae may look like simple creatures," he told me, "no more complicated in their anatomy and habits than mere nematodes or the simplest of annelids, but genetically, it's a very different story. "They need to retain so much potential, for the eventual shaping of the imago—which is, of course, much more complex anatomically. Bringing out some of that potential while the larva is still a larva isn't difficult, in engineering terms, if you have the necessary switching skills. Even Mother Nature sometimes retains the option of doing that, in connection with phenomena such as paedogenesis, where larvae develop reproductive organs normally seen in the imago. Building better woodworm to add the final touches to gantzed structures is so straightforward that it's become standard architectural practice, and the early refinements I made were simply the next logical step in that direction—as you've obviously deduced from a superficial study of the body of the house."

His tone suggested that I hadn't gone beyond the obvious, and I felt a trifle insulted by that. "That's the context in which England's insect engineers have explored giantism," I observed, "but the giant larvae that are conventionally used to tunnel through gantzed compounds and native rock aren't capable of reproduction or metamorphosis. They're produced to order, to work and then die."

"That's because the imagoes that would emerge if the larvae pupated would be unviable," he remarked. "They'd be incapable of breathing or of locomotion, because the necessary kinds of modification hadn't been made to their potential."

"But you've done better?" I queried, rhetorically. "Your borers *can* reproduce, either paedogenetically or by producing viably imagoes?"

"That's right," he said. "I can show you that process in various stages of progress—maybe tomorrow, if I can make time. There's a sense in which it's not strictly necessary for my borers to be able to reproduce, of course—the familiar industrial models do the job—but the project fell so neatly into the scope of my general research that I slotted it in."

"So the relative sophistication...the artistry...of your borers was as much a side-effect as an actual target of your research?"

"You could put it that way," he replied, in a slightly evasive fashion that was becoming slightly irritating. "The humble servants that helped to hollow out my rooms were faithful companions for some years, and I have a certain affection for them, but yes, the development of their artistry—and I approve wholeheartedly of your use of that expression—was a sideline to less orthodox experiments unconnected with their vulgar purpose."

"Artistry is never superfluous," I told him, "except in the Voltairean sense that the superfluous is a very necessary thing."

"You're quoting again, Peter," he pointed out.

"Unrepentantly," I assured him.

He passed his hand over his face. He seemed tired again and somewhat strained. I knew that he'd been working all day, and was therefore entitled to a certain weariness, but I suspected that there was something else involved in his sudden brief fits of apparent near-exhaustion.

In view of what we had said before, the first hypothesis that sprang to mind now was that his condition must be due to the lingering after-effects of some psychotropic compound.

"How much Aether are you taking, Rowland?" I asked him. "And why are you continuing to take it, given that its side-effects seem to be causing you some distress?"

He seemed surprised that I had noticed; he had obviously been trying to hide the symptoms, and had imagined that he was succeeding. His first ploy was to say: "It's nothing."

"It's *not* nothing, Rowland," I told him. "*Something*'s going on. Why can't you just tell me about it? We're friends, after all."

He hesitated, but must have decided, in the end, that I was right. "I've used unorthodox methods of brain-stimulation in the past," he confessed, eventually. "There do seem to be some belated side-effects—but they're treatable. Aether's not the cause, but it does seem to be an adequate solution—until something better comes along."

"By *unorthodox methods of brain-stimulation*, do you mean intelligence-enhancers?" I asked slight surprised. So-called intelligence enhancers had been around in pill form for more than a century, and had been one of the most fashionable products of experimental engineering labs for a brief period long before Rowland and I had been born, but the vogue was long past...unless current research on olfactory psychotropics was abut to revive it.

"Not exactly," he said, reluctantly.

"Then what, *exactly?*" I persisted.

""I've experimented with a number of methods," he said, still being determinedly and unhelpfully unspecific. "I never gave up on the experiments we began as students. I started work on olfactory psychotropics at the same time as Rosalind, but didn't find olfactory delivery as satisfactory as she seems to have done. The stuff reaches the bloodstream rapidly enough, and the dosage is easy to control and even out, but some of the compounds that Rosalind and others have tried to develop in that context need better targeting."

"Better targeting?" I repeated. "By vectors of some kind, you mean? Please don't tell me that you're dabbling in cerebral somatic engineering, Rowland. The reason it's illegal is that it's highly dangerous. You might persist in referring to your brain as *the old tumor*, but it's...."

I stopped dead. Maybe the expression on his face had tipped me off, or merely it was a pure stroke of inspiration, born of a more general context, but I guessed what he had done, even though it had never been done before.

"Oh no," I said, reluctant even to voice the idea that he had used his own cerebrum as a target for some kind of somatic transformation, which had inevitably misfired. Had he learned nothing from Professor Fliegmann's cautionary tales regarding the limits of practical neurology?

Eventually, I bit the bullet. "You really are ill, aren't you?— and not in any familiar way. Is that why you didn't come to Magdalen's funeral? Is that why you're no longer communicating with your mother or your sisters? I thought you were just distancing yourself, they way I've distanced myself from my father...."

"I'm just *busy*," he told me, insistently. "I have work to do. Nothing's wrong with me. I invited you to stay, didn't I? Whatever you're imagining, it's not true. I'm just a little tired. I've been using stimulants like Aether for a long time, partly to keep me going and partly, I admit, in the attempt to enhance my creativity...but it's nothing that people haven't been doing for centuries by drinking *coffee*, damn it!"

"But you've been targeting the doses," I said, reminding him of what he'd already conceded. "You couldn't be content to entrust the stimulants to your bloodstream—you've actually introduced new genetic material into your brain to increase its sensitivity. You used some kind of transformation vector, didn't you? You've deliberately given yourself some kind of artificial brain tumor!"

"Mention of brain tumors isn't helpful," he said—hypocritically, given that he was probably the only person in the world who made a fetish out of referring to his entire brain as a tumor. "I haven't infected myself with something that's growing, let alone out of control, threatening to disrupt the working of the brain. The augmentation isn't producing pain, or delusions, or causing amnesia. It's just a supplementation of the neuronal network, at a key point in the cerebral labyrinth. It was experimental, obviously...but I'm not a idiot, Peter. If necessary, I can kill off the supplementary cells at any time, in a matter of minutes, with a single magic bullet—but that's not necessary and it's not desirable.

"It really has helped me...and if it occasionally makes me a little wearier than I would be without it, and a little more haggard in my facial expression, then so be it. That's no price at all to pay for the kinds of benefits I've reaping these last ten years. It has nothing to do with my not being able to attend Magdalen's funeral, or my lack of communication with my mother, and I'm astonished that you, of all people, might think that it had. Of all the people in the world, Peter, I thought you'd be able to understand."

Fair trade, I remembered from my reverie of the previous evening, is an illusion. Although it's commonplace, psychologically, for both parties to a deal to think that they're coming out ahead, when you look at the deal from an objective standpoint, one of them is always being screwed. Exploitation is the norm. Rowland obviously believed that he was exploiting whatever "augmentation" he'd introduced into his brain—but the situation might look different, from an objective point of view.

"Why didn't you tell me about it, if you were so sure I'd understand?" I demanded, trying to keep all bitterness out of my tone.

"I just have," he said—again, hypocritically.

"Have you set up *any* kind of independent monitoring?" I demanded. "Or are you allowing your neotumor-infested brain to be the sole judge of what the neotumor-infestation is doing to it?"

"That's a gross distortion of the facts," he told me, coldly. "You're talking like a second-rate horror story. I have an expertise in these technologies more advanced than anyone—more advanced that Rosalind, even. What I did hasn't been done before, but I've been careful all along, and it hasn't given me a moment's anxiety in all these years. I don't need anyone to look over my shoulder—that's not why I brought you here."

"*Brought* me here?" I echoed, sharply.

"Invited you here," he corrected himself. "Oh, I know you think that you inveigled me into inviting you, just as I'm perfectly well aware that you wouldn't have take the trouble if Rosalind hadn't given you a shove, but the simple truth is that you're here because I wanted you here—but not to lecture me on the dangers of self-experimentation and practical neurology. I wanted you here—I *brought* you here—because I thought you might be able to understand, eventually, what I'm doing. I knew that it would take time—maybe months—before you'd be able to get your head around it properly, but you're my friend, and you're Peter Bell the Third, and I thought that you, unlike Rosalind or any of my little sisters, *might* eventually be able to understand."

Oddly enough, I didn't put that little rant down to the fact that he'd been screwing with his old tumor. I'd seen and heard its like many times before, although I'd needed to see and hear its like again to be reminded of how delicate Rowland's temper could be. Again, I felt that I had been transported back in time, and my reaction came from then as much as now.

"You're right, Rowland," I told him. "I do need time, sometimes, to get my head around things properly, to understand some kinds of things fully—and I ought to have known that you weren't fooled for a moment by the apparent spontaneity of my call, and my angling for an invitation. Rosalind did give me a shove—but I'm not here on her behalf, and I really do want to understand what it is you're doing here. And I *am* your friend."

I had always had to emphasize that fact, back in the day— as if neither of us could quite believe it. He was my friend too, just as implausibly, from an objective viewpoint. And no matter how implausible it might have been, from a supposedly objective viewpoint, it was a mutually beneficial and dedicated symbiosis, in which neither of us was getting screwed.

Rowland sat back in his armchair, almost as if he were relieved to be able to let his weariness show now that the reason for his strange condition was out in the open—or, at least, no longer completely obscured.

"Where were we, before we got sidetracked?" he said. He meant, where had we been in the discussion of abstruse scientific matters—but I wasn't prepared to go back quite that far, as yet.

"Wouldn't it be a good idea," I asked, "if you were at least to let someone else look at your scans? Not me—it's not my specialty—but an expert neurologist?"

"No," he told me, "it wouldn't be a good idea. An expert neurologist might detect something he hadn't seen before, and he'd jump to the conclusion that, because it didn't fit his preconceptions, it must be bad. He'd have his magic-bullet gun drawn before you could say 'snipe.' The scans don't matter, I'm living in here, Peter—if there were anything wrong, I'd know it."

That, of course, was exactly the point. Because he was living inside his old tumor, with its relatively new modification, he might be in the worst position of all to judge the risks he was running, or even the effects to which he was subject. He was taking Aether to counteract the lingering side-effects, after all, and although Aether was supposed to be entirely safe in the context of normal brain tissue, the reason he felt that he needed it was precisely that his brain-tissue was no longer Mother Nature's unadulterated product.

There was no point in persisting, though; I knew how stubborn he could be. If he was prepared to take months preparing my unaugmented brain to accommodate whatever secrets he was hoarding in his bizarre dwelling, the least I could do was invest some time in preparing his augmented brain to accommodate the need to obtain a second opinion as to its efficacy and security from harm.

"I'm just worried about you," I said, all too conscious of how feeble I sounded.

"I'm *not ill*," he insisted. "In fact, I'm better than I ever was. I've barely scratched the surface of my ambition, but I've already achieved enough to ensure myself of the kind of immortality that Roderick achieved. I fully expect to live for another two hundred years, and maybe more, but no matter when I die, this house, or her descendants will outlive me. If I can bring about a successful metamorphosis, she might live for millennia—but long before then, she'll be producing paedogenetic offspring that will revolutionize generic engineering. Rosalind's branch of the Usher family will doubtless thrive, thanks to her own ectogenetic children and grandchildren, unto the umpteenth generation, but the House of Usher and her kin will be still be one of the wonders of this world when our descendants have built new worlds around distant stars. How's that for *Romantic imagination*?"

I had told him once, many years before, that it had been his "Romantic imagination" that had initially drawn me to him. He had refused to take it as a compliment.

"I may be the clone of solid-state physicists," I told him, "but I've done everything I can to cultivate and care for my own Romanic imagination. I can compete with the best when it comes to waxing rhapsodic about the futures nascent in the genetic technologies of today, vaulting across future centuries with talk of the miracles that the godlike genetic engineers of the far future will work—but I still have my feet on the ground."

He smiled at that, wryly. "No you don't," he said. "You're in the House of Usher now, and you have no idea what lies beneath your feet—but I'll show you, in due time, and I'll help you to understand, fully."

He was so weary by now that his speech was becoming slurred—and that kind of incapacity was something he obviously did not want to display. Before I could reply to his last challenge, he announced, abruptly, that he needed to go to bed—but that he would try to make some time the following day to show me a little more of the house and its wonders.

CHAPTER TWELVE

The hour before I retired to my own bed I spent reading. On the shelves in my bedroom I found a box of memory-sticks containing records of Roderick Usher's experiments, and some of Rosalind's too, but I wasn't tempted by offerings of that sort, and might not have been tempted even had Rowland taken the trouble to include records of his own work, selective or otherwise. Instead, I sought solace in more familiar works loaded on to my own bookplate—the poetry of William Blake and Lord Byron, and (how could I avoid it?) Edgar Allan Poe. I say *solace*, but I really mean distraction, because my recent conversation with Rowland really had given me cause for extreme anxiety. The storm outside was dying down now, but as I looked back mentally over the day, I was struck once again by the remarkable effectiveness of the insulation provided by the house.

I had not quite realized the extent to which Rowland had cut himself off from the world, by retreating into a house that he evidently imagined as a kind of maternal womb. No doubt he went outside on a regular basis, and not just to unload and distribute supplies from the quayside or harvest his plantations, but even his further ventures were mere excursions into wilderness and solitude, with no human contact. With the exception of Adam and Eve, he seemed to have placed all his social relationships in suspended animation. Marvelous as it was, could the House of Usher really be reckoned a healthy environment, in psychological terms?

I was not afraid on my own account, of course—I had every

confidence in my own psychological resistance—but I would have been afraid for Rowland even if he had not vouchsafed his revelation about the supposedly-benign tumor that he had deliberately implanted in his brain in order to feed his imagination with even more recklessness extravagance than Mother Nature had provided.

Perhaps it was my reading-matter, and perhaps it was the residue of my discussion with Rowland, but I felt a slight and subtle shift in my experience of the house. Although it was almost silent, and fully proof against the gusts and vibrations of the wind, the smooth, warm walls that surrounded me no longer seemed quite as comforting as they had when I had stood at my window that morning, reveling in my immunity to the storm.

When I finally lay my head on my pillow I suspected that I was in for a turbulent night, full of vague nightmares in which the imagery of Eddie Poe's poems would mingle with the dreams and achievements of Rowland Usher's Conqueror Worms, who would continually triumph in an uncertain, unnamed tragedy— from whose toils I would not escape until I awoke, perhaps in a cold sweat, several hours later but long before the dawn.

The last part of the prophecy was true, but no sooner was I fully awake than I was no longer able to remember whether there had been any truth in its more Romantic aspects. I reached for the bedside table, on which I had placed a glass of water, and put it to my lips. My hand seemed steady enough.

No sooner had I taken a sip of water, however, than my attention was caught by a sound in the corridor outside. Although there was nothing sinister in the sound itself, I felt a prickling sensation run down my spine, and my heartbeat suddenly accelerated.

Don't be silly, I told myself. *If you can't remember a nightmare, it's ludicrous to let its emotional aftershocks reverberate.*

That was perfectly reasonable, but when I heard the sound again, it drew a gasp of pure terror from my throat.

There is nothing to fear, I quoted to myself, *but fear itself.* Sometimes, innovation is the last thing we need, and habit is healthy.

I knew perfectly well, on a rational level, that I ought not to be afraid, so I deliberately got out of bed. Then I forced myself to go to the door and open it. Such was my querulous state of mind, however, that it was only by the merest crack that I pulled the batten ajar, and as I peeped out into the corridor my irrational heart still was pounding in my breast.

The corridor was not quite dark, although its bioluminescence was considerably toned down, so that what remained was a faint radiance—which was bluish now, not ruddy, as before. Because the corridor curved I could see only a few meters in either direction, and could see only one other door—that of Rowland Usher's bedroom.

That door too seemed to be ajar, but there was darkness within. Moving away from the door, though—just disappearing from sight around the gentle angle of the tunnel—was a human figure. I caught no more of the merest glimpse of it, but I had the distinct impression that it was a young female, perhaps fourteen or fifteen years of age. She was quite naked.

Eve? I thought—but that was ridiculous. Eve was in her thirties, and dark-skinned. In the blue-tinted light she would have seemed almost black, like a gleaming shadow. The person I had glimpsed had been pale—almost as pale as a ghost.

It was the word *ghost* rather than any impression of recognition that called forth the next absurd hypothesis.

Magdalen?

Again, I told myself not to be ridiculous—that Magdalen too had been in her thirties when she died—but barely had the syllables of the thought been sub-vocalized in my mind than I flung the bedroom door wide open and set off down the corridor in pursuit of the phantom.

I was barefoot, and the floor of the corridor was as soft as the walls; I ran without making the slightest sound. Had anyone seen me, they would doubtless have come to the same conclusion I had reached on glimpsing my quarry: that I was a phantom, whose very existence was absurd—but no one saw me, and no one came after me. She it was who fled from me down the labyrinthine ways, as if I were the Hound of Hell.

I didn't catch her. How could I have caught her, since she couldn't really exist? But I did glimpse her again, on three more occasions, just as she as about to disappear again around a curved in the spiral corridor that led down to the lower floors of he house. The tunnel had forks, but I thought I knew them all, and thought that I was close enough behind her not to mistake the route that she had taken—but somehow, I must have missed my way, or hers, because I lost her, eventually, and ended up in the vestibule inside the main door, confronted with the doors of the store-rooms and the two elevators.

I was sure that she hadn't opened any of those doors. She was, after all, a ghost. It would have been easier for her to pass straight through one without opening it—but I was certain that she hadn't done that either. How? I don't know—but I was certain…just as certain as I was that, if the phantom really had been a phantom, then it must have been the phantom of Magdalen Usher, come to haunt the brother she had loved—in the end, fatally—more than she had been able to love me.

I wondered whether Rowland had seen her, and decided that it was unlikely. He had been very tired; he must surely have been fast asleep. Perhaps the ghost had stood beside his bed and leaned over him; perhaps she had reached out to plant a dream in his weary head—not a nightmare, but a pleasant dream, a luxurious nostalgia.

Yes, I thought, if Magaden really were a ghost now, this was the house that she would choose to haunt. And if ironic Fate had allowed her to do that, it would surely draw some amusement from the fact that Rowland had not seen his sister on this occasion, while I had. It was not me that she had come to haunt, but I had loved her too, unrequitedly. Rowland had been loved in return, but had felt the eyes of the world and his mother upon him, as had Magdalen, and they had fled the mutual attraction: a voluntary abandonment. My loss had been of another kind. How apt, then, that I should see Magdalen's ghost slipping out of Rowland's bedroom, where he lay fast asleep, in order to pursue her, fruitlessly, through the labyrinth whose twists and turns I had obviously not yet mastered in full!

That was too much. I pinched my arm violently, to make sure that I was awake. The pinch hurt, and raised a welt. I was definitely awake. In order to prove it to myself, I took the stairs back to my room rather than taking the short cut via the elevator or the long way round via the spiral ramp. My feet made no sound on the stairs, but I felt them as I hoisted myself up from one to another, ascending by degrees.

The pointlessness of it all seemed suddenly overwhelming. Deserting Rowland, after a few months spent in the bare bones of the house, had not solved Magdalen's problem. Separation had killed her. Frustrated love had killed her. Regret had poisoned her, perhaps with a little chemical assistance. Rowland had suffered too—that was obvious. As for me…I was so stupidly prey to my residual feelings that I had just raced through a labyrinth in pursuit of her ghost, even though I knew that what I had seen—what I continued to see, at intervals—could not possibly be real. I hadn't even recognized her; it was desire, and desire alone that had summoned Magdalen's mirage into my mind.

It is better to have loved and lost, I told myself, sternly, *than never to have loved at all*—but I didn't believe myself. I believed Sophocles. *The best thing of all is not to be born, and after that to die young.* Anyway, I hadn't really loved and lost, had I? I had only yearned, longed, desired and driven myself mad with stupid obsessive infatuation…I had never *really* loved, because I had not been loved in return. But Magdalen had always been so *kind.* She had not even done me the bitter favor of spurning me, of explicitly rejecting me. She had always been my friend, albeit in a very different sense from the sense in which Rowland had always been my friend. She had always been elusive, continually glimpsed but somehow never really there.

I closed my bedroom door behind me and got back into bed, but I sat up straight momentarily, in order to take another sip of water.

I wondered briefly whether the water might have been drugged, but rejected the notion as yet another absurdity. I told myself that I would be perfectly all right in the morning....

And so I was.

When I woke up again, and showered, I felt all the craziness of the night flow away and disappear, leaving me serene. The idea that Rowland's sister Magdalen had somehow risen from the dead became the indulgent Romantic fancy that it was—a sport of the imagination. The power of rational thought, exercised in the warm light of the tropical dawn, enabled me to dispel the idiot fancy, and to feel a cool breath of welcome disgust at the fact that I—a pragmatic scientist of the twenty-second century—had allowed myself to be briefly infected by the morbidity of the Gothic Imagination.

I cursed Rowland Usher and his absurd termitary of a house, but I was only blowing the last of the night's cobwebs away. I didn't mean the curse. Had Rowland been at breakfast when I arrived in the dining-room, I would have greeted him with sincere warmth. In fact, there was no one there at all—but I had been shown where all the supplies were, and could fend for myself.

I stared idly out the window while I ate, noting that the weather was still a little blustery, though not longer authentically stormy. It was still raining, but the rain was morose now, rather than fierce, almost as if it were conscious of the fact that it could not long endure. So, at least, my personal version of the pathetic fallacy interpreted what I saw.

I was on my second cop of coffee—dilute, milky coffee—when Rowland finally appeared. He seemed quite well, and cheerful too, so I set aside all possibility of asking him, even in jest, whether he might conceivably be being haunted by the ghost of his near-twin sister.

Rowland told me that he had time enough, that morning, to continue the guided tour of his abode, promising glimpses into some of its remoter nooks and crannies, and so we soon set forth yet again into its amazing winding corridors.

He paused to showed me several other guest-rooms—none of which showed the slightest sign of ever having been inhabited—and several further storerooms, some of them crammed with collections of objects that he had obviously inherited from past generations, as well as hoards of his own, but we both knew that any time spent on the upper floors was effectively wasted. Not that the collections were devoid of interest. There were antique books for which there was no room on his study shelves, some with acid-rotten pages that should have decayed a century ago, some even dating back to the nineteenth century. There was a collection of minerals, one of old medical specimens, and one of ancient navigational instruments—all inherited, I suspected, from generations even remoter than Roderick's

When we eventually descended into the lower strata of the house I found things much more coherently organized, and considerably more interesting.

"I probably shouldn't show you the most important of the laboratories yet," he told me. "I've a great deal of explaining to do before you'd be able to understand what I'm doing. I'll show you some of my early work, though."

I was hoping that we would go down below as far beyond ground level as possible, so that I could at least form an estimate of the extent of that part of the house, but we only went down to the first subterranean floor, which was almost indistinguishable from the floor directly above it. Rowland did show me some laboratories—rooms full of sequencers where he had once conducted extensive endeavors in genomic analysis, and rooms fitted out for the transformation of gantzing bacteria—but none of them seemed to be in current use. They belonged to his past; he had moved on. The equipment they contained was modern, but it would not have been reckoned "state of the art" even by mortals far lesser than Rosalind—Professor Crowthorne, for example.

His fermenters were all in use, growing bacterial cultures, but fermenters are essentially unspectacular. Rowland's were more interesting than others I had seen because they were built into the fabric of the house, but that was a mere design detail. I saw more giant insects, but none significantly more exotic than the ones I had already seen on higher floors.

Rowland talked a great deal, offering information as to what the equipment he showed me had been used to do, and what tasks it was still performing, but there was little explanation in what he said. He seemed determined to let his precious secrets out slowly—more, I suspect, because he was so used to clinging on to them than because he really feared that I would be slow to grasp their intellectual essence.

I memorized the route down to the first subterranean level, though, and took note of doors that might yield access to lower ones.

In return for all the information that Rowland vouchsafed, I marveled audibly that any one man could possibly make use of such extensive laboratory facilities, and complimented him repeatedly on the achievements he had made. He assured me that the high level of automation made it reasonably easy to operate his machinery and maintain his cultures. He had relatively few household robots, regarding the motile varieties as inherently unreliable examples of the mechanician's art, but admitted that some routine activities were contracted out to service personnel who operated machines by remote control.

"I suppose that I should train Adam and Eve to offer more assistance on the scientific side," he said, "but I prefer them in their present roles. That's selfish of me, I know…but I think they prefer it too. If either of them were specifically to request…but the simple fact is that things are as they are."

He showed me other holding tanks in which he kept his various species of burrowing "worms", which interested me more than anything else I had seen, because of the previous evening's conversation. Most of the species needed special containers, made of some substance that they could not break up or digest, so there was more metal and plastic here than in other specimen-holding rooms. There were observation-windows that let us look in upon the creatures in opaque containers, although we could see little enough within because of the difficulties of providing lighting systems immune from the ravages of the larvae.

Rowland told me that he allowed a few species of these "worms" to live freely in the structure of the house, as parasites, because they were too limited in their habits to damage its structure, and performed useful waste-disposal functions as they foraged for food.

"You'll run across one of them sooner or later, in one of the corridors," Rowland told me. "It might give you a shock at first, but you'll soon got used to it. Please don't tread on them, deliberately or accidentally."

"How do you direct the burrowing of the more voracious species?" I asked him. "Surely, any kind of escape would be desperately dangerous—some of the worms must be able to devour the fabric of the house."

"Elementary cyborgization," he told me. "The creatures have little or no brain, and are guided through life by simple behavioral drives. It's a relatively easy matter to fit their nervous systems with electronic devices that deliver the appropriate commands by electrical or biochemical stimulation. I handle them with great care, mind. They can't live on the materials they're designed to tunnel through, and their diets are deliberately exotic. I feed them what they need in order to execute a particular task, and no more. They can't escape, and couldn't live in the wild, so to speak, if they did."

Watching those curious creatures, whether roaming loose or imprisoned in their tanks, made me slightly nauseous, although I had often seen their smaller kin before. Most were like monstrous blowfly maggots—big and soft and white, their body walls so transparent that one could see the organs inside them. Some of them were a meter and a half in length and at least eighty centimeters in girth. Their internal organs were not conspicuouly colored, but they were wrapped in complex webs of blue and pink. Rowland told me that he had equipped their bodies with defined circulatory systems, in which hemoglobin-laden ichor circulated, in order to serve the oxygen-needs of their organs; like us the creatures had deoxygenated blue ichor in their veins and oxygenated red ichor in their arteries.

Some of Rowland's "worms" looked more like elongated centipedes than maggots, being bright yellow in color and equipped with hundreds of pairs of limbs along the length of their plated bodies. These too were the largest of their kind I had ever encountered, being at least four meters long, although only as thick as a man's wrist. A few of the living machines were, on the other hand, surprisingly small: there were black, hard-skinned creatures that were only a few centimeters from head to tail, though they had vast heads that were almost all jaws. Rowland informed me that these were very difficult to rear because of the enormous amounts of food they had to consume in order to work the massive mandibles. In their holding tank, they were virtually submerged in high-protein fluid.

"Perpetual life in the womb," I observed. "Born for rare brief intervals, and the returned. Every embryo's dream."

"Do you think so?" he said, as if I'd meant it seriously.

"Of what else can an embryo dream but an eternal, or near-eternal womb?" I suggested, flippantly. "How could it imagine the potential rewards of life after birth, even after having fallen into that hell repeatedly, to perform allotted tasks?"

"But it's not an embryo," he objected. "It's a larva."

"The principle," I insisted, frivolously, "is the same. It's the way of life that's important, not the exact biological status of the liver."

He nodded. "Sorry," he said. "Slow on the uptake—I see what you mean."

But I wasn't sure that he did, given the way he was living himself.

CHAPTER THIRTEEN

The marvels of the tour had a cumulative effect, as we moved from room to room, and my initial frustration evaporated. Rowland showed me clusters of "roots" that the house extended into the substrate of the swamp, and the apparatus for gathering in organic materials from the silt. He showed me further examples of the biological batteries that produced electricity for his research laboratories—which had a potential output, Rowland boasted, equivalent to thirty billion electric eels. All I saw of such systems, however, were their superficial termini; most of their mass inevitably remained hidden; what could be seen of the house's systems was far less, in metaphorical terms, than the tip of an iceberg.

Rowland assured me that there was still more to be seen, and than the full tour would require at least one more day. He reeled off statistics in an impressively casual manner, telling me that the biomass of the house was greater than ten thousand elephants, and that if it had been a single organism then it would have been the vastest that had ever existed on Earth.

As the time afternoon wore on, however, it was evident that Rowland was once again becoming increasingly tired. His graphic descriptions began to diversify into flights of fantasy, in which he repeated himself without apparently being aware that he was doing so—but they did extend further than the beginnings laid down the previous day.

I listened to his prophetic ramblings, to the effect that houses descendant from this one would gradually replace the plants and animals making up the world's ecosystems in the course of the third millennium, so that in a thousand years' time the entire ecosphere might well consist of nothing but organic artifacts: not merely houses but entire cities, all of which would be locked into a careful mutually symbiotic relationship, controlled by humans or their successors.

"Successors? I said. "Post-humans, you mean?"

"If you like," he replied—but the remark was a mere punctuation-mark in his flight of fancy, and he obviously disapproved of my interruption. In a world such as the one he was anticipating, Rowland hypothesized, sexual reproduction might become the sole prerogative of humankind, if humans survived at all, everything else in the organic realm being capable only of vegetative growth or of being cloned and transformed by genetic engineers—but only if the masters of the ecosphere wanted it that way.

I got the strong impression that he wouldn't, if he were the master of the ecosphere: that houses descended from his would be sexual mothers in every sense of the world—more so, although he was careful not to spell it out in those precise terms, than Rosalind, who had to make elaborate use of *in vitro* fertilization and ectogenesis in producing her children.

I confess that I did not find his vision of a world full of living houses a wholly attractive prophecy (or speculation, for Rowland was talking of opportunity rather than destiny) but there was, as ever, something very attractive in the sheer grandiosity of Rowland's ecstatic voyages of the imagination. The magic of his ideas took a firm grip on me, encouraging my own mind to the contemplation of vistas of future history extending toward infinite horizons. I joined in with his game for a while, and briefly became so carried away that I didn't notice immediately that Rowland was so very tired that he was having difficulty supporting himself.

I couldn't believe that showing me around his petty empire was any more physically exhausting than the work he routinely did in his laboratories, but Rowland definitely seemed more distressed than he had at any time during the previous two days. After the previous day's argument, I didn't want to labor the point, but I felt that I had to forbid any further wandering when we were still more than an hour short of diner time. Diplomatically, I told him that I was tired and needed rest, and he seemed grateful that I had taken the trouble to spare his feelings.

Once dinner was served, however, the food seemed to revive Rowland's body and mind alike, and he ate heartily. Afterwards, he seemed sufficiently restored to commit himself to conversation again, in the comfort of the study, with another bottle of wine.

He set out, initially, to tell me more about the history of his researches, but we soon moved on yet again—quite naturally, it seemed—to more intimate personal matters. I didn't have to make any effort to steer him toward the subject of Magdalen, which seemed to be exactly where he wanted to go.

"She should have come back here," he said, flatly. "I deserved that. Whether we could have worked things out or not, she should have given me the chance. She owed me that much. She should at least have kept in touch with the work, and continued talking to me about serious matters, instead of mere trivia."

"Perhaps she didn't consider the things she wanted to talk about mere trivia," I suggested, softly. "She was worried about you, as I am…and Rosalind too. If you were as dismissive of her anxieties as you are of mine, that probably made her worry even more.

Tellingly, his reply was: "She had no cause to worry about me. Evidently, I was the one who had cause to be worried…but I didn't know that. She knew how busy I was, but if she'd given me any hint that she was in trouble…more trouble…."

"Perhaps she knew what you'd say," I offered, hesitantly. "Perhaps she knew that you'd only urge her with all your might to come back here—and didn't want to do that."

"But it's what she should have done," Rowland persisted, "whether she wanted to or not. Given time, I could have explained.

Given time, I could have brought her back into the work, shown her what we needed to do, taught her how we needed to go about it. She was brilliant, you know, in her way. She never thought so, but she was. She was Rosalind's daughter—and my sister. I tried so hard to get her past the obstacles that were in her way. If she'd only stayed, or come back…."

"Perhaps she needed you to go to her," I suggested. "Perhaps, if you'd been willing…."

"That's Rosalind talking," he said, flatly—and quite unfairly, I thought.

"Just because she's your mother," I said, in a voice that was hardly above a whisper, "it doesn't mean she's always wrong."

He contrived to laugh at that, although I wasn't at all sure that I'd intended it as a joke.

"Don't take her side," he said. "You're my friend. You're supposed to side with me, even if you can't quite understand yet what this is all about."

"I loved Magdalen too," I said.

"I know—but she wasn't your sister."

"She was your half-sister," I said, "and even Rosalind says, now, that she could have coped, and would have supported you, if…."

"Don't be absurd," he retorted. "She's lost a daughter, and is entitled to a little foolishness after the fact—but you know full well what kind of effect it would have had on the family, the Hive, everything, if we'd ever be able to reconcile ourselves to it…which we couldn't."

"In which case," I said, quietly, "what would have been the point of her coming back here?"

He shook his head, but didn't bother to tell me out loud that I didn't understand. "Do you think Rosalind has ever had sex?" he asked me, abruptly.

I was shocked as well as startled. "How should I know?" I retorted.

"I didn't mean with you," he said, misunderstanding the alacrity of my reaction. "I meant with anyone."

"I knew what you meant," I assured him. I wanted to change the subject, but I didn't dare. Absurd as the question was, he'd asked it with certain intensity. For some unimaginable reason, he thought that it was important. "It's none of my business. I imagine so. Just because she didn't go that route to have her children doesn't mean that she doesn't do it….and certainly not that she's never done it."

"I don't think she ever has," Rowland opined, brutally. "I don't think anyone could ever be good enough for her, except the one man with whom it was out of the question."

This time I was astounded. "Roderick?" I said, incredulously.

"Exactly," he replied.

"Are you sure you're nor projecting your own feelings on to her, wanting to co-opt her into a similar confusion?" I asked, rather rudely—but we already seemed to have left the limits of diplomacy far behind.

He laughed, though, and said: "Maybe. Sorry—this is making you uncomfortable isn't it? Although you'll need to understand everything, in the end. In my youth, you know, while Rosalind and I were still on speaking terms, she told me about one of her grand plans—trying it out for size, as it were. You're only familiar with the grand plans she's actually put into operation, of course, but there were many others that fell by the wayside. The one thing I'll always be thankful to her for is my imagination. Anyway, the grand plan was that she wanted to free humankind from the burden of sexual attraction, and direct our capacity for love into more appropriate channels—and she meant it, quite seriously."

The one thing I couldn't possibly say was that it didn't sound like such a lousy idea to me, so I tried to formulate a sardonic laugh instead. "Can I have three guesses as to what the more appropriate channels might be?" I asked, flippantly.

"You'd only need one," he told me.

"Flowers?" I suggested, knowing that I'd almost certainly hit the nail on the head.

"Absolutely," he said. "Can you imagine it: on-line catalogues of floral sex-aids? Sweetly-perfumed, of course, and as lovely to touch as to look at?"

I could imagine it easily enough—what I couldn't imagine, though, was that such outlets would every command the loyalty of a significant minority of humankind, let alone the entire race. "Actually," I told him, "I'm not sure that she's given up on that particular dream. She might have accepted that marketing flowers designed as masturbation-aids was a non-starter, but her research in olfactory psychotropics might have been inspired by the dream of cutting out the middleman—or middlething—entirely."

"Olfactory orgasms," Rowland mused. "Yes, that sounds like Rosalind's sort of dream. I doubt that it's possible, though."

"You shouldn't underestimate possibility, Rowland," I said. "Just because she's your mother...."

"You've already done that joke once," he said, interrupting sharply. Obviously, he wasn't prepared to laugh at it a second time.

The moment was becoming awkward, and I cast around for a way to break the spell.

"I had a dream last night," I said, hesitantly. "At least, I think it was a dream. I thought I saw Magdalen's ghost."

"Where?" he asked, in a determinedly neutral tone—so determinedly neutral that I couldn't tell what emotion he was trying to keep out of it.

"Here. I chased her round and round the spiral corridor, but I couldn't catch her. In the end, I lost her."

He paused for three exceedingly long seconds before saying: "I sometimes dream about her myself. More than sometimes. Often. More often still since I got the news."

"Understandable," I opined.

"Understandable," he agreed. "You too—understandable, that is. Even Rosalind...."

"Please," I said, "no more discussion of Rosalind's sex life, or lack of one."

"Right," he said. "Insensitive. Sorry. How on earth did we get on to it in the first place? My fault, wasn't it? You must forgive me. Spending so much time on my own, I've got into the habit of talking to myself—my internal censor's dropped its guard. I'll have to remember, now that I have company more intimate than Adam and Eve, that I need to think before I speak—or at least before I change the subject. We should be taking about sensible matters: gantzing, genetic transformation, the management of control genes, *house-building*. We were talking about those sorts of things, weren't we, before we went astray?"

"It's okay," I said. "We're friends. We can go astray occasionally. It doesn't matter." I didn't want to suggest that it might not have been a lapse in his internal censorship that had led us astray—that it might, instead, have been the effects of his self-induced tumor—because I didn't want to make him angry, and because I didn't want to say that even to myself, privately.

"You're right," he said. "It's harder to slip back into the old relationship than I thought it would be, isn't it? Sometimes, everything seems so easy, so natural, but then....we suddenly realize how long it's been, and that time hasn't stood still in the interim. We have time, though, don't we?—time to rediscover what it was that made us such good friends, back then."

"Yes," I said. "We have all the time in the world."

I thought it was true.

CHAPTER FOURTEEN

"Do you see your father at all, nowadays?" Rowland asked me, even though he'd observed only a few minutes before that we ought to be talking about rational and constructive matters, about what made the world tick and how its clockwork could be adjusted to bring about a better time.

"No," I said. "He and I don't move in the same social circles any more. People think geneticists are mad, because all our discoveries seem unnatural at first, but it's the physicists who cling most obsessively to their own asylum and speak entirely in tongues. He took it hard when I deliberately went my own way. I'm a clone, after all. He'd hated his own father, but at least he'd fought him on his own ground. He could have understood it if I'd hated him in the same way—but to walk away entirely, to wash my hands of him, to take up genetics…there's only so much a clone-parent can stand. And only so much a clone-child can take."

"If there were a Peter Bell the Fourth," Rowland observed, "you could direct the development of the embryo much more cleverly than he did. You wouldn't have to do any genetic transformation—just give the control genes a little nudge, aiming for a better balance in the initial set-up of the cerebrum."

"Why?" I said. "Don't you think I'm perfect as I am?"

He didn't laugh. "None of us is perfect," he said. "Mercifully."

"Mercifully because we'd have nothing to strive for if we were?" I queried.

"No," he said. "Quite the opposite. If perfection were possible, we'd know what we were striving for, and we'd probably find a way to achieve it. Far better for perfection to be impossible, flaws inescapable...or, at the very least, for everyone to disagree as to what would count as perfection."

"According to theoretical physicists," I said, quoting something I'd read, which my father certainly hadn't written, "the universe itself is imperfect. Their continued failure to find a unifying theory isn't the fault of their observational and experimental technique or mathematical ingenuity—it's the fault of the universe, and its dogged refusal to make sense. I'm not sure how they can claim to know that, but they're physicists, after all."

"We all do it," Rowland said.

"Do what?"

"Project our own perceived faults on to others—including the universe. Why haven't you ever amounted to anything, Peter?"

"What?" I said, outraged by the insult even though I could see why he might think that I hadn't.

"When we were young," he said, forgetting that we still were, "we seemed to be on the same wavelength, equally intelligent, equally imaginative—but now you're a teacher, collecting marine alga, looking for trivial chimerical anomalies. You've never *attempted* anything. You're still a physicist at heart, looking at the world and trying to understand it, but not involving yourself in it."

He was allowed to say such things because he was a friend, but I wasn't going to take it lying down. "Unlike you," I said, "living in the middle of a reconstituted wilderness, making yourself a new mother because you can't get along with the one who didn't want to give birth to you because it didn't give her enough control of your destiny, and shaping her as a vast glorified womb. You've really made something of yourself. I'm not quite sure what it is, mind, but it's certainly *something*."

"Touché," he said. "If only you'd ever managed to lash out at your father like that, or I'd ever got that kind of grip on Rosalind...do you think we'd feel a little better about ourselves?"

I shook my head, tiredly. "I doubt it," I said. "They wouldn't take it in the same hilarious spirit as we do, of course, but they'd still laugh it off. We're their children, after all."

"And neither of us would ever have dreamed of saying anything similar to Mag, would we?—even though she's the one who really didn't make anything of herself at all."

He just couldn't let it alone. How could he? I was only here because Magdalen was dead; how could we keep the thought of her out of our minds for long, no matter how determined we were to throw ourselves into our work, into our safely scientific obsessions? Whatever we had come to, we had come to it because of our love for Magdalen: the love that we couldn't have, but couldn't bring ourselves to live without…except that we *had* lived, after a fashion, without it. Magdalen was the one who hadn't. Magadelen was the one who had actually summoned up the guts to kill herself.

"She shouldn't have done it, though," I said, in a low voice.

"Made something of herself?" Rowland queried, not having been privy to the train of my thoughts.

"Killed herself," I said. "She should have carried on. She should have done *something*, made *something* of herself—built her own crazy house, rather than going back to living in the bosom of Rosalind's. However imperfect our lives are, they *are* lives." I hesitated, momentarily, but then plunged on: "It wasn't our fault, Rowland, was it? It wasn't because of the way we handled things…both running away…that left her with so little that, in the end…."

"Don't flatter yourself," he said, brutally. "No, it wasn't your fault. No, it wouldn't have mattered a damn if you'd tried to so something different, found some way to be or behave that would have changed her mind. I'm the one who killed her, not you."

I felt suddenly guilty about putting the idea into his head. "You mustn't think like that, Rowland," I told him. "She killed herself. If it's self-indulgent for me to try to blame myself, it's just as self-indulgent for you. I shouldn't have put it as a question. It *wasn't* our fault, Rowland. She was the one who ran away, from you as well as me. She killed herself."

"No, Peter," Rowland said, in a voice that was pure desolation. "Rosalind lied to you…or let you believe the false conclusion to which you jumped. Magdalen didn't kill herself. Rosalind let everyone believe that because it was preferable to letting the truth be known—or what she thought was the truth. I don't know whether she figured out the whole of it—Mag certainly didn't—but either way, she had grounds for sending you here to torment me. In a way, if not quite in the way that Rosalind thinks, I *did* kill her."

I was completely out of my depth. I had no idea what he was talking about. "But you've been here all the time, haven't you?" I said, hesitantly. "Magdalen died in England—in Eden. You couldn't possibly have killed her. Rosalind said that she was poisoned….in circumstances, if I remember her words correctly, that made it highly implausible that it had been a accident, and that it certainly wasn't murder."

"Very scrupulous of her," Rowland said. "Avoiding the word suicide in order to direct attention to it. Kind of her too, in a way, though not entirely. Accident and murder highly implausible, were they? But she *was* poisoned, in a way. Rosalind chose her words as carefully she chose her messenger…but nobody could accuse her of being a pedant. I know how Magdalen died, Peter—and I know why Rosalind sent you here. I know why you came, too, so there's no need to protest against the last remark. You came because you wanted to, because I'm your friend. I know that. But she still sent you, and I know why. She's wrong, but also right. I'm sorry, Peter—I won't say that I'm sorry that you got dragged into it, because you were always in it, and you're entitled to know the truth."

That was when enlightenment finally hit me—belatedly, it seemed, and I cursed myself for a fool because I hadn't caught on earlier, although, in retrospect, I had been handed the essential piece in the jigsaw very recently, and out of context. At any rate, I realized, all of a sudden, what he was talking about.

I didn't blurt it out, though. My lips actually felt numb; I couldn't speak. The revelation came in a single surge, not in dribs and drabs. I understood how and why Rowland had killed his sister. I understood why Rosalind had sent me. And I understood why Rowland was sorry.

"You and I first met when we were eighteen," Rowland said, his voice weakening almost to a whisper, as if the process of distant recall required him to lapse into trance-like reverie. "Magdalen was eighteen too, of course—we met you at the same time, although I don't know which of us saw you first, or which of us you saw first. It doesn't matter. You didn't know anything about us, except for the fact that we were Rosalind's children, and we liked that—we liked it about all the people we met, of course, but we saw something of a kindred spirit in you that we didn't see in others. Superficially, at least, your upbringing had been similar to ours: like us, you'd never been to school, but had been educated at home, according to a strict regime that had a particular end in mind…ends against which, not surprisingly, we had all rebelled.

"In the beginning, Peter, I admired you, because I thought that you had taken your rebellion further than ours. Eventually, I realized that the appearance in question was superficial…but I still admired you for succeeding in it, and saw myself in you, as you must have seen yourself in me, perhaps with a little admiration thrown in. I'd always had Magdalen, and Magdalen had always had me, but you didn't seem to have had anyone. I think we befriended you thinking that you might need us—the sort of support that we'd always been able to provide for one another—and we really did want to be kind, but in reality, we needed you more than you needed us.

"You were already self-sufficient, but the fact that we were brother and sister made our mutual endorsement of our own eccentricity seem suspect, a potential *folie à deux*. We needed someone outside ourselves to pass favorable judgment on us, and you did that. You never withdrew that favor, either—never, even when you realized that falling in love with Magdalen had been futile, because she was too intimately bound up with me ever to return your love. You never turned against us, even when it became obvious that we hadn't done you any kindness at all—quite the reverse."

"That's not true," I murmured. He ignored me.

"You weren't the only one to fall in love with Magdalen, of course," he continued. "How could you be? She was beautiful. She won the admiration of everyone, merely by her appearance, and there was nothing in her character to alienate that affection. She was charming, and she was good. There was no malevolence in her at all. Nobody who loved her could turn that love to any kind of distaste, even though she couldn't and didn't return it.

"Perhaps we simply didn't rebel sufficiently against the grand plan that Rosalind had mapped out for our lives. I don't mean that we should have abandoned genetics for solid-state physics—that would only have been a small sidestep, and it would only have been a reaction against the part of the plan of which we were consciously aware. We didn't realize, you see, the extent to which our own relationship had been planned. My mother had produced non-identical twins with different fathers deliberately, not in pursuit of some puerile symmetry but because she wanted to provide each of us with what she considered to be an ideal companionship. She wanted us to become a self-sufficient atom of community, as tightly bound as the proton and electron of a hydrogen atom.

"Rosalind actually set out, in supervising our upbringing, to build such a bond of affection and intimacy between us as to make us the lights of one another's lives. I'm not saying that she actually intended that the bond in question would be literally incestuous—in fact, I suspect, implausible as it might seem from an objective viewpoint, that she never actually thought about the possibility of a sexual element, because she sincerely believed that, as brother and sister, we'd have no need of any such complication, and that no feelings of that sort would every materialize. If she had anticipated the possibility, she would have dismissed it as a minor irrelevancy—something not worth worrying about. I suspect that she'd never had any strong feelings of that kind herself—that she'd successfully repressed any that had threatened to arise in the course of her own unorthodox upbringing—and that she simply took it for granted that we wouldn't either.

"I suspect that, looking back on her own childhood and adolescence, Rosalind was only conscious of one defect, one lack. She had been an only child. She had felt an absence of a companion like herself. It must have seemed to her that the kind of uniquely close companionship that she tried to develop in her own first-born children was the greatest treasure that any human life was capable of discovering. She never said that to us, though; we thought of it as ours, as an aspect of our rebellion against the more obvious ways in which she tried to direct us. We tried to isolate ourselves from her, in the interests of psychological survival, but we didn't try to isolate ourselves from one another—indeed, our collaboration became the heart and soul of our reaction against her, enabling us to present a unified front in every act of defiance, petty or otherwise.

"Rosalind must have realized very swiftly that her experiment was going awry. Mag and I were eight before she decided to have another child, but even at that early stage she must have been dissatisfied with her experiment, because she didn't plump for another pair of twins, and never had another son thereafter. When we were at university—as I undoubtedly told you—I thought that was because she thought the downside of masculine genius too dangerous, to closely akin to madness. She might even have told me that herself one day, when she was trying to teach me and I was trying not to learn. There's probably even some truth in it...but I'm not sure that it was the real reason, even if the events that brought us to this could be interpreted as a vindication of that excuse."

What he meant by that was that an uninformed observer might think that it was, indeed, the masculine or quasi-autistic aspect of his genius that had brought him to the Orinoco delta, prompting his seclusion as well as his bizarre experiments with giant insects and the living house. An informer observed of the single additional fact that he had killed his sister—or believed that he had—would have been even more convinced of it. I knew, however, that he wasn't mad, and that the worst charge that could be leveled against him was that he had been reckless, and unnecessarily so. He had made a mistake—but I never imagined, even for a moment, that he had made it without Magdalen's informed consent.

He was undoubtedly the one who had used a transformation vector to implant twin benign tumors in their forebrains, but they must have collaborated in the experimental design, and Magdalen must have insisted that if he were to try his experiment on himself, then he must try it on her too, simultaneously. He was evidently convinced, now, that it was the tumor that had killed Magdalen—perhaps because he suspected that his own tumor was about to kill him, having reach a similarly critical stage in its unexpected development—but he didn't actually know that to be the case. For all he knew, Rosalind might have been telling the exact truth, her implication being straightforward instead of sly. Magdalen really might have swallowed poison. I knew that I would have to put that to him at some stage, if only to persuade him that he need not die in his turn—especially if he consented to obtain an expert second opinion as to what was going on inside his brain. For the time being, though, it seemed best to let him continue his monologue, which obviously still had some way to go.

"Rosalind over-reached herself in trying to bring us up in the image she wanted us to become," Rowland went on. "You and I can hardly blame her for that, though. Our ambition always raced far ahead of our capabilities, in those days, and I dare say that it still does—I apologize for implying, a little while ago that yours had fallen behind, for I really have to idea of what is going on in your head, and haven't yet given you the opportunity to tell me. Perhaps her plan to create a perfect partnership, and her plan to perpetuate her own ambition, both succeeded too well. At any rate, the difficulties that materialized in my relationship with Magdalen gave us both a reason to exercise our powers of creativity, and perhaps to overstretch them. I don't say, now that I have hindsight to aid me, that our attempt to solve our predicament was sensible—but it was its very boldness, its very recklessness, that drew us to it.

"It wasn't so very original, I fear. Two hundred years ago, people who found their own feelings—their own lusts—inconvenient, uncongenial or hateful sometimes tried to suppress or redirect them with the aid of psychotropic drugs, operant conditioning, electroshock therapy and brain surgery. My plan was much subtler than that, and, I thought, much cleverer. I was arrogant, of course, perhaps stupid—and perhaps Magdalen should have stopped me instead of encouraging me—but we really thought that Rosalind's mistake could be corrected.

"We weren't, of course aiming to do anything as simple as obliterate the sexual feelings we had for one another. What we wanted to do—or at least, the way we represented it to one another and ourselves—was to enhance our powers of reason, the dominance of thought over notion, in the interests of achieving the kind of calm of mind that Platonic philosophers recommend as the ideal....for philosophers, at least. We wanted to be great scientists, and I thought that there might a short cut to the attainment of that ambition. Nor am I convinced, even today, that I was entirely wrong about that—for I *am* doing great work here, Peter, as you'll understand when I've explained it in full, and shown you its dearest fruits."

I couldn't take any more.

"You gave her a brain tumor, Rowland," I whispered. "You gave your own sister a brain tumor, in the hope that it might somehow allow her to rise above or set aside the feelings that were supposedly getting in the way of her intellect. No matter how good a deal you think you've made on your own account, do you have any idea how monstrous that is, from an objective point of view?"

"Of course I do," he replied. "That's why I gave her the placebo. I thought that would be enough. It was only a matter of exorcising an illusion. I thought it would be enough to persuade her that I'd done it. I was prepared to try the real experiment on myself, but not on Mag. Not on anyone else."

Yet again, my assumptions came crashing down—for once, an ugly hypothesis slain by a fact that, if not beautiful, had a certain weird elegance about it.

I thought I understood everything, then—or almost everything. I thought I understood why Rosalind had sent me—and why, although she was wrong about what had killed Magdalen, she was also right.

"Rosalind doesn't know that you gave Magdalen a placebo," I said. "Does that mean that Magdalen still didn't know, even at the end?"

"That depends what you mean by *know*," he said. "As soon as I was convinced that the placebo effect hadn't worked—that her feelings were just as intense and confused as ever—I confessed to Mag what I'd done. The trouble is that I'm not sure that she ever believed me. She should have one, because she knew me. You believe me, don't you, Peter?"

I believed him. But I could see why Magdalen might not have done.

"Oh what a tangled web we weave," I muttered, helplessly.

"You're quoting again," Rowland pointed out.

I didn't care. I understood, now, why even Rowland, who had actually done nothing at all to Magdalen, imagined that he had killed her. He had put a belief into Magdalen's head, and then had been unable to free her of it by means of a mere confession that the belief was false.

Rosalind had sent me to accuse him, without knowing what I was doing. And I had, without knowing what I was doing. It hadn't been necessary. Rowland was already accusing himself, even though he knew exactly what he hadn't done. A tangled web indeed.

"It didn't work, did it?" I said.

"Obviously not," he said.

"I don't mean that it didn't work on Magdalen—I mean that

it didn't work on you, either. You really did try to give your own brain a nudge, but it didn't work. You still loved Magdalen. You still do."

"I never really expected it to work on me in *that* way," he said. "I did hope for the results I actually got, though, and I'm more than willing to settle for those. The lust thing was never really an obstacle for me, in the way it was for Mag...or, as it seems to have turned out, for you. It never stopped me thinking, or working. As you say, I still loved her...but I'm thinking, and working, harder than ever. If Mag had only come back, I could have convinced her, in the end. I could have proved to her that I hadn't done anything to her. I could have helped her over the obstacle some other way. Rosalind couldn't, you see—and no matter how much it pisses Rosalimd off that she couldn't, that's the truth of it. Mag should have come back...but Rosalind wouldn't let her. It's fair enough, though, that Rosalind should blame me, rather than herself. However you slice it, I did it. I set the wheels in motion. Ultimately, no matter how you weigh it up, I caused Mag's death. I didn't mean to, but I did do it."

I wasn't about to contradict him, to tell him that Rosalind was really to blame. I don't even think he was fishing for the contradiction. What I actually said was: "It might have been a lust thing to you, but for her...and me...it was *love*."

"Call it what you want," he said. "No need to glorify it, though—it's still just one of Mother Nature's nasty little tricks, not something we should wallow in."

"You really are your mother's son," I murmured, "no matter how much you dislike her."

"Maybe," he conceded. "Unfortunately, Magdalen wasn't quite her mother's daughter. In retrospect, the placebo effect never had a chance. She always believed that the experiment would fail, in her case if not in mine. She wanted to free herself from the victimization of her emotions, as her mother seemed to have done, but she never believed herself capable of it. She went back to her mother, I think, in the hope that her mother might enable her to succeed where I had failed. It was difficult for her, because she thought of it as a betrayal—as, indeed, it was—but she thought it necessary at the time, and I dare say that Rosalind has done her best, with her own methods and placebos.

"I can't claim that I achieved the philosophical calm of mind that was my ultimate objective….but that doesn't mean that I consider the experiment a failure. Perhaps calm of mind is underrated, even by philosophers. Perhaps great science… and all great achievements of any kind…really do emerge from mental ferment and suffering, as Romantic artists claim. I have, at least, made every effort to channel all my own feelings into my work….and you'll be the judge, when you're ready, of the extent of my achievements.

"I can say, I think, in all honesty, that I'm proud of what I've achieved, and justifiably so. I don't regret having stayed here after Magdalen left, at the expense of becoming a recluse, accepting separation from the society of science and family alike. My memories of Magdalen have always seemed far more precious to me than any other relationship with a woman or a man could ever have been. In fact, her death ought not to make much difference now, for I've long grown accustomed to her absence…in a material sense, that is. There's another sense, as you've observed, in which she's still here, in spirit and ambition…."

The monologue finally faded away—not, I think, because he had no more to say, but because the weariness had overwhelmed him again

I was trying hard to come to terms with the implications of what he had been saying, even though it was difficult, if not impossible, for me to put myself imaginatively in his shoes. At the level of feeling, however, I couldn't help a certain resentment, partly at the fact that neither he nor Magdalen had ever told me what they had planned to do, but mostly because they had not invited me to take a part in the plan.

That wasn't because they believed me to be already possessed of an adequate calm of mind, obviously. Why was it, then? Had we not been close enough, as friends, to entitle me to their confidence? I wouldn't have agreed, of course—but perhaps I would have been able to talk them out of it. Perhaps, in fact, it was for that very reason that they hadn't told me. Perhaps their silence had been a compliment of sorts. Or perhaps not.

I remembered the apparition of the previous night, which I had already mentioned to Rowland, obliquely, but of which I still feared to speak. I couldn't help but touch upon the subject again, but felt compelled to do so as elliptically as before, without revealing exactly what I had seen, imagined or felt.

"She *is* still here," I said. "I can sense her nearness, more acutely here than I could in Eden, when Rosalind delivered her eulogy."

Rowland got up then, and went to the sideboard where he kept his alcoholic beverages. The wine-bottle from which we had been drinking was empty. He didn't pick up another bottle, though. Instead he rummaged in a drawer for a bottle of pills, shook two out into the palm of his hand and swallowed them.

He turned to took at me, and said: "Just Aether. Crude, in spite of all the efforts chemical engineers have put into the engineering of better psychotropics—but effective. Not as subtle as Rosalind's perfumes, of which she'd be only too happy to send me samples if I asked, but…well, tonight, I need to stay awake. I have work to do."

"You can't possibly…," I began, but broke off. Who was I to tell him what he could and couldn't do, in is own house?

"I'll see you in the morning," he said. "I'm sorry for being boring. When I get tired, my mind wanders. Tomorrow, we'll get back to real subjects—in the evening, if you're going to spend the day collecting algae downriver. We'll get down to some serious genetics, at last."

Without waiting for a reply, he strode out of the room. I remained sitting in the study for a further ten minutes or so, but it seemed very empty without him. Eventually, I returned to my own room.

This time, I was careful not to read before I went to bed, but I did look out of the window for a while. The rain had stopped, and the sky was clearing. It was going to be a fine night, and if the weather held, the next day might indeed be ideal for collecting specimens.

I went to bed early, and tried not to think too much about the conversation we had just had, in the interests of peaceful and dreamless sleep.

CHAPTER FIFTEEN

There was no sign of Rowland at breakfast the next morning. I asked Eve whether she had seen him, and she shook her head—but she seemed totally unconcerned by his absence, and was obviously well used to his keeping highly irregular hours.

I thought, given that the good weather had held and that the sky was blue from horizon to horizon, that I might as well do what Rowland had suggested and go out in a boat with Adam, taking advantage of the favorable circumstances to explore the surroundings and collect some of the local algae.

I loaded a considerable number of bottles and jars into the smallest of Rowland's three boats—the only one powered by an old-fashioned internal combustion engine rather than a bioelectric motor, but much speedier in consequence—and eventually filled them all, but without paying overmuch attention to what it was that I was picking up. In the main, the excursion was a petty voyage of exploration, allowing me to figure how the local land and water lay.

From a distance, the environs of the house had looked like jungle, the predominance of the greenery giving the impression of a vast forest, but at closer range, the true extent of the water became clear. Very few of the mangroves visible from the upper windows of the house were actually rooted in solid ground; the majority were growing in shallow water. At ground level, the strips of land seemed narrow and the squarer patches small; the impression given by the landscape as a whole, save for the channel through which the ferry had brought me on the first day, was of swampland.

There were, however, channels of deeper water, which Adam seemed to know very well, and he was able to guide the boat through a labyrinth at least as complex, and far more extensive, that the one within the house, in order to point out what he considered to be the salient features of the delta country. He showed me trees and he showed me flowers; he even pointed out birds and insects, on occasion. He tried to show me algae, having been apprised of the fact that my interests lay in that direction, but he had obviously paid very little attention in the past to the weeds cluttering up the navigable channels, regarding them purely as a nuisance to be avoided or cursed, and he was unable to direct my attention to anything of significance.

It was difficult to see the fish in the brackish waters, but there obviously were fish there, because we did see a small Orinoco crocodile at one point. Crocodiles and their near relatives were one of the few groups of larger vertebrates to have come though the Crash without drastic species loss—as was perhaps to be expected, given that they had come through so many extinction events already in their long evolutionary past.

The aftermath of the storm had left the air a little fresher than it might have been, but my sojourn inside the house had allowed my body to begin the process of physiological adaptation to the tropical climate. I sweated far too profusely, and the sun's fierce rays burned my skin even though I was wearing a wide-brimmed hat and a long-sleeved shirt. I couldn't stay outside for very long without further practice. It didn't seem to matter; I had all the time in the world.

We returned to the house at about noon, and I transported my desultory collection of specimens to the lab, where I spent the afternoon making an initial inspection and classification. I found nothing unusual to suggest that the kinds of evolutionary processes that I'd briefly mentioned to Rowland might be going on hereabouts—but I knew that I'd have to look a great deal harder, and exercise considerable patience, before I could hope to turn up evidence of exotic responses to the crisis.

When I went up to dinner, however, Rowland was absent again—and this time, when Eve replied in the negative to my enquiry as to whether I had seen him, she seemed a trifle anxious.

"Perhaps you should go look for him," I suggested, "to make sure that he's all right."

"You come," she said—so I did.

I steeled myself for a long trek, but in the event, we didn't have to look far. It transpired that Rowland was in his room, in bed—and this time, his condition had clearly gone beyond mere fatigue.

"I'm all right," he assured me, when I rushed to his side—but he clearly wasn't.

"How long did you work last night?" I demanded.

"I had things to do," he retorted. "The necessities of the task set the timetable—you know that. I'm tired, but I can't sleep. It's the Aether—you know how it is. The pills do the job, but the ingenious chemists haven't quite got over the problem of the let-down effect when the drug wears off. The after-effects are sometimes inconvenient. I'll be fine—and I'm *not* addicted, even psychologically. It's just a busy period, nothing more. Get me a glass of water, will you."

I fetched a glass of water from the bathroom, and then went to ask Adam and Eve to prepare some food for him that he could eat from a tray without getting up. I ate with him, from a second tray balanced on a small side-table. The food seemed to revive him somewhat, but he seemed slightly feverish.

"You're not well," I told him. "I think you ought to put yourself through a full medical examination and send the results to a Med-Center for analysis."

"I will," he promised, meekly. "First thing tomorrow."

I settled for that, and moved my chair back to the bedside in order to sit with him.

"I need to bring you up to date," he said, after an interval of silence. "Not that anything's going to happen but…just in case."

"Okay," I said.

"Bring me the portable screen from the desk, with the hard keyboard from the top drawer. I can't use a virtual on this coverlet."

I did as I was told.

Bringing me up to date, at least for the first couple of hours, consisted of explaining how his files were organized and how to access them. "It's all here," he told me, "and all in order. All the data, that is. As for the explanations...well, I was hoping to take you through the whole chain of inspiration, step-by-step, but maybe it would be as well to give you a summary first. You need to know, after all...if anything *were* to happen, all this would be yours."

"What?"

"You didn't think I was going to leave it to Rosalind and the Hive, did you? My will's on file in Caracas and London—there won't be any problem."

"Your will's on file? Even though you're perfectly all right and expect to live to be two hundred? And you've left your bloody house to *me?* Your house made of silt in the middle of the Orinoco bloody delta?"

"Don't be childish, Peter. Who else could I leave my scientific legacy to? That's the important thing, of course—although the millions might come in handy, especially if Rosalind were to try to challenge the will. Not that I expect her to do anything of the sort—she wouldn't stoop *that* low."

"You're frightening me, Rowland."

"I frighten myself, sometimes," he admitted. "Now sit down, and listen. This is the heart of the matter."

I sat down, and listened—pointlessly, for at least three minutes. He had closed his eyes, but not because he was about to go to sleep. He was gathering his thoughts. In spite of the fact that he had resolved to tell me his secrets, starting with *the heart of the matter*, I think he was still hesitant. Indeed, I don't believe that he would have told me any more at that point in time had he been in full possession of his faculties—but whatever he said about not being addicted to the Aether he was using, coming down from its effects was obviously having a drastic effect on him. He had planned a more gradual process of revelation, but he hadn't made elaborate plans for any synoptic summary of his endeavors of the last ten years. He was more than slightly confused—but in the end, he began.

"The first thing I need to make clear," he said, "is that I never had any plan to duplicate Magdalen, or build any kind of simulacrum. That wasn't the point. I began the work before she left, not knowing that she was going to leave—believing, in fact, that we would see the whole plan through together. Eve was with us even then, but it never occurred to us to carry out a full genomic and proteonomic analysis of her make-up, let alone start culturing her tissues. How could Eve have given informed consent, in any case? Magdalen was always the model we were going to use. *We*, not me. I don't want you reading anything untoward into the plan, the way Rosalind probably would… probably has, if Magdalen told her about it."

"I'm not following," I told him. "You'll need to make yourself a little clearer."

"I'm getting there!" he retorted. "Listen, will you. Even after she had gone, no matter how much I missed her, I never planned on re-creating her, or creating some kind of substitute. That wasn't why we started working with the larvae, and it wasn't why I continued. You remember, obviously, how fascinated I always was by the phenomenon of metamorphosis, by the genetic mechanisms that permit insects to live two sequential lives, as very different organisms. You remember the work we did, even as postgraduates, on the biology of pupation. Mother Nature's finest conjuring trick: the creation of tombs that are also wombs."

"I remember," I told him, and quoted: "Give me a larva large enough, and a pupa with real leverage, and I'll shift the gears of creation."

"Did I say that? It certainly sounds like me. Structural engineers were already inducing giantism in various kinds of boring larvae, of course—prototypes of the ones we were looking at yesterday—so I had a head start in that aspect of the work; it was easy enough to transfer the techniques to other kinds of larvae. It had always struck me as a terrible waste that structural engineers should be designing and breeding hundreds of new kinds of larvae to work for them, without sparing a thought for the fact that their eventual pupation would be effective death—that nothing could ever emerge from their tomb-wombs but unviable monsters, if anything emerged at all. The journeyman gantzers didn't care, of course—they just ground down the stillborn-corpses for their chitin and processed the slush into culture-feed. No one was putting in the work that would allow giant larvae to produce viable imagoes…imagoes that would, of necessity, have to resemble vertebrates more than the simple exoskeletal forms that insects usually adopt."

"And you figured that if you were going to use any kind of vertebrate model, you might as well shoot for the jackpot," I said, putting two and two together with the usual consummate ease. "Why bother with crocodile-beetles or bird-moths, when you might as well go all the way, and produce insect humanoids?"

"I knew *you*'d understand," he replied, although the slight sigh of relief he emitted suggested that he hadn't been entirely sure. "At any rate when I began engineering larvae for work within my house, I also began engineering them so that they would be able to pupate and metamorphose successfully. You'll probably have taken note that the largest of the larvae I showed you yesterday—the ones with networks of blood vessels—had approximately the same biomass as an adult human being. They lose much of that in pupation, but they can still produce something the size of a child, or even a young adolescent.

"The imagoes are mindless creatures, of course, and I can't honestly say that they could pass for human in daylight, let alone for any specific human—but they *are* beautiful, in their way. I might be biased, but I think they're even more beautiful, in their own way, than human beings. Just because Rosalind's my mother, as you keep reminding me, it doesn't mean that she's always wrong, and she's not wrong about the fact that insects and flowers alike really were selected *to be beautiful*, in accordance with some sort of universal aesthetics. If ever the mimics were to compete with authentic human women...but that was never the point."

"Mimics?" I queried.

"Insects are good at mimicry," he reminded me. "They already have that kind of potential built into their control genes. It was easier than I thought, once I got the trick of it. If only Mag had stayed a little longer, to see the early successes...we'd accelerated the generations, of course, but insects are good at that too. They're not all prisoners of the calendar. The downside of that acceleration is that the imagoes don't live long, at present—only a few days, for the most part—but the project is still in its early stages. I've laid the foundations for work that has limitless scope. In time, the engineers of the future might produce another human race—a hundred more human races. The imagoes won't be mindless forever, you see. I'm generating tumors wholescale, but you can imagine how difficult it is to produce even the rudiments of a brain by means of that kind of trial and error.

"If I'd started with fish, or even snakes, my chances of generating a shark-brain or an anaconda-brain would probably have been much better, but I didn't...and anyway, there are other organs to develop too. Eyes weren't so difficult, oddly enough, once I'd done the transformations to lay on the proteinaceous raw materials—almost as easy as skin and hair. Liver-substitutes, pancreas-substitutes and the like are much, much, harder, but once the outward appearance and internal bone-structure—or, for the moment, chitin-structure—are in place, the guts will follow, step by step...and the brain too. Enough tumors, enough generations, and the guts and brains will form. It's just a matter of engineering and selection. All it needs is time. And we have all the time in the world, don't we, Peter? I have the word of your inner cliché-factory on that, don't I?"

"Yes," I told him, with utter insincerity. "You have all the time in the world. And I understand your reasons for making Magdalen a model—but why the only model, Rowland? If I'm taking the right inference from what I'm hearing, all your mimics are female."

"That's right," he said. "Sterile of course....not equipped, as yet, with any kind of reproductive apparatus. All workers, no queens...and no drones. In time, though...God got it backwards, of course, in *Genesis*. First you make your females, equipping them, in the first instance, for parthenogenetic reproduction... you only need males if and when you decide to add sex into the equation, to shuffle the genetic deck, and you only need to do that if and when you want your new human race to be capable of natural evolution, of finding its own future destiny.

"Honestly, do you think there'd be any point in that? Don't you think they might be happier if they don't have to get involved with all that crap? Don't you think they'll have a better chance at Utopia if they're all female? We have genetic engineering now, and directed evolution. We don't need Mother Nature's crazy makeshift any more...*they* won't, at any rate. They'll be much better off without it, don't you think? What has sex ever done for us...for you and me, I mean...except screw us over?"

"I think we might be exceptions to the rule," I said, quietly. "Rosalind's son and Peter Bell the Second's clone...it was never going to be easy, was it, to adapt ourselves to that side of human life? But think of the beauty—the human beauty—we'd be missing, without sexual desire, sexual longing, unrequited love—and requited love too, for those fortunate enough...."

"The Romantic imagination," Rowland said, even more scornfully than usual. "There *is* beauty, Peter, without the sublimation of the sex urge. There *is* an objective aesthetics. Insects might not know that consciously, and flowers certainly don't, but even so, they *are* beautiful. And you didn't answer the question. Even if we *are* exceptions to a general rule—and I think the rule might have far more exceptions than you suspect—what has sexual desire ever done for you and me, except cause us pain and make us miserable?"

"It didn't have to be that way," I murmured.

"In a better world, Magdalen might have loved you back," Rowland said, voicing the thought behind the thought, "and in the same better world, I might have loved someone else too. But *this* is the world we're in, Peter. *This* is the world we have to change…and if we can't change it by ourselves, as we probably can't, we have to prepare the way for those who will.

"Mother Nature fucked it up, Peter; the insects were trapped into slavish dependency on flowers, instead of going on, instead of exploring the potential rewards of metamorphosis to the full—but we can make a difference. You and I can make a difference. I want you to promise me that if anything does happen to me, you'll carry on. I want you to promise me that you'll be my heir—not for the sake of the millions, but for the sake of the future."

"What about my algae?" I said.

It sounded stupid even to me. I could have told him that I didn't have his genius, his imagination, his sense of purpose, his artificial tumor, but I wasn't about to admit that I was anything less than he was. I had loved her too, at least as much as he had, at least as much as any other human being could have done. I had been bereft for a decade too, and now that she was dead, I knew that all hope—even illusory hope—was extinct. But all I could actually say, for the moment, was: *what about my algae? What about my work?*

"You can't let me down, Peter," he said. "You mustn't—for Magdalen's sake." A low blow, that one.

"I can't let you down because I'm never going to get the chance," I told him, wondering that I could even form the syllables of such an outrageous lie. "You're going to live for another two hundred years…perhaps forever. We might be members of the first generation whose members don't have to die, Rowland—except, when they somehow come to wish it, by their own hands. We have all the time in the world."

I really was tempting Fate in saying that—but the last thing in the world I expected Fate to do was take me at my word, with hardly a moment's delay. Even in the absence of solid-state physical causality, things sometimes come together. There's not only an objective beauty in the way of the world, but an objective irony too. Sometimes, when Mother Nature fucks things up, it's not an accident, whether we can see an explanation or not.

Rowland hadn't been consciously afraid, and he'd had good reasons not to be. He'd already told me that he could demolish the supplemental cell-network that he added to his cerebrum with a magic bullet—a virus tailored to destroy those cells and no others, by targeting a gene incorporated into them precisely to make them vulnerable—and do so at a moment's notice. To be quick on the draw, though, you have to be determined, and you have to be ready. You can't fire while you're in denial, obsessively telling yourself that you're all right, that you're going to live forever….

And you can't fire, either, if your real intention, conscious or unconscious, is to die. Roland had let go of his secret now, or as much of it as he was ever going to yield. He had made his will. Perhaps it was only the privileged custody of his secret, his refusal to see or speak to anyone but his innocent Adam and Eve, that had kept him alive for so long. Rosalind had, after all, expected him to die first. He was the one who had literally screwed up his brain; Magdalen had only received the placebo. He was the one who had rendered himself physically oversensitive to the effects of Aether; her vulnerability was purely psychological, beyond the reach of rational consciousness and natural science.

I could see all of that, in my mind's eyes, but none of it mattered, for the moment. What mattered was that Roland was no longer merely ill, but dying. Something in him had shattered or dissolved—not directly because of anything I'd said to him or he'd said to me, and perhaps not even directly because of Magdalen's death and the dire poison of regret that it had suddenly injected into him, but simply *because*….

Rowland suddenly began to cough, explosively, as if a gob

of saliva had slipped into his windpipe while he was trying to swallow. I patted him to the back, then grabbed the glass of water from the side-table and tried to put it to his lips. The cough developed into a kind of seizure—by which time it was far too late to think about the Heimlich maneuver. That only works with solid objects, anyhow.

I reached out to him with both arms and tried to calm and comfort him—but blood spattered my right hand, and I realized that the seizure wasn't passing off, wasn't stopping. His face had a ghastly pallor, and he struggled to whisper.

"Magdalen!" he contrived to say, pronouncing her name in full, if not very clearly-enunciated. "I'm sorry...."

It was as if the words themselves asphyxiated him, although he wasn't actually choking. I tried to clear the non-existent blockage from his throat, in order to administer artificial respiration, but I couldn't start his heart beating again, once it had stopped.

Within minutes, he was dead.

CHAPTER SIXTEEN

I sat with the body for a couple of minutes, having no idea what to do next. I didn't call Adam and Eve. Eventually, I picked up my phone and did the only thing I could—not in the sense that it was the only thing that was theoretically possible, but in the sense that it was the only action of which I was capable, at the time. It was the only action that would let me off the hook.

I called Rosalind.

"It's Peter Bell the Third," I told her answer-AI, although she would have knew that perfectly well, as my caller ID would be automatically displayed and she'd be able to see my face when she played back the message. "Rowland's dead. I'm sorry. He had some kind of fit—I think the proximal cause of death might be a cerebral hemorrhage, but it was probably brought on by an anomalous reaction to Aether, caused by some kind of somatic modification he made to his brain ten years ago. An autopsy will probably clarify the matter."

She returned the call within two minutes. She didn't curse me. She hadn't even gone pale. It was almost as if she had been expecting it—as she probably almost had. She, after all, was probably the only one who knew exactly how Magdalen had died, and probably had her own secet ideas about exactly how the responsibility for her death had to be divided up.

"How long ago?" she asked.

"Five minutes…maybe ten, by now. No more than twenty."

"I'll be there as soon as I can," she said. "You'll have to connect the body to all the appropriate machinery, for the medical analyses, but I'll take care of the legal formalities *en route*. I'll seal this connection, but you'll have to put an access code into his system. Can you do that?"

"Yes,"

"Is he in bed?"

"Yes."

"Good. You do have nanoprobe equipment and scanners on hand, don't you? *He* has, I mean?"

"Yes."

"Good. Once the hook-ups are in place and I'm in control of his system, you can leave everything to me. It's about eight p.m. there now, yes?"

"Just after. That makes it midnight where you are?"

"Just after," she confirmed. "It'll probably be late afternoon tomorrow, at the earliest, by the time I can get there, even though I'll gain four hours in flight—a long wait, I fear. Thanks for calling right away. You did the right thing."

Mother Nature might have been able to match Rosalind for creativity, but she'd never had that kind of organizational flair.

I had to tell Adam and Eve what had happened in order to send Adam in search of the various medical apparatus needed to hook the body up to the house's systems and launch the automatic autopsy. Giving control of the house's systems to Rosalind was easier.

Adam and Eve took the news hard. Adam checked Rowland's body very carefully for signs of life, just in case, but found none.

Finding Eve's alarm and grief harder to bear than my own, I left her to sit with the body while the post-mortem examination was carried out, although I made sure that Adam was able to operate the scanner before leaving them to it.

I made my way back to the study first, where I sat at the terminal for a while, monitoring Rosalind's operations. She seemed to be handling "the legal formalities" with ruthless efficiency, but I didn't suppose she was doing it all personally. Rosalind knew how to delegate. The only thing I decanted for my own use was a three-dimensional map of the house, but I didn't put it to immediate use. I tucked it away for future reference. I did locate and check out Rowland's own copy of his last will and testament, which confirmed that I was now the owner of the House of Usher—or would be, once the will had gone through probate.

The will requested burial of the body beneath the house, and the subsequent recycling of its organic material by the house's systems. That wouldn't have been legal in England, but this was Venezuela, and a region of that crippled nation beyond the reach of any surviving law. I didn't suppose that Rosalind would be happy about it, but I decided that I would have to insist if she tried to object, because that was what Rowland would have wanted me to do—and I didn't want to start debating with myself, as yet, as to exactly how far I was or wasn't prepared to go in doing what he wanted me to do.

It was past eleven when I finally went back to Adam and Eve, to make sure that they knew that Rosalind was handling everything, and that they mustn't do anything but wait. Then I asked Adam to dim the house lights and returned to my own room. Midnight had gone by the time I got into bed, but my inner sense of time seemed to have become confused, and I didn't begin to feel tired until I actually made a conscious decision to go to sleep.

Then, fatigue suddenly swept over me like a wave. I wondered if that was how Rowland had felt in the wake of his brain-tempering. I wasn't tempted to go looking for his Aether supply, though. I wanted to go to sleep.

With darkness and fatigue, though, came an inevitable relaxation of reason, and when I did go to sleep, my self-control—so carefully maintained during the last few hours by the iron grip of determined consciousness—was banished. I dreamt more nightmarishly than I had done on any previous night of my life, and my dreams were pure Eddie Poe.

I dreamt that I buried Rowland not in his own house but in the other House of Usher—the haunted purgatory of Romantic fantasy. Our long journey to the grave was through rotting passages weeping with cold slime, lit only by smoky torches whose flames were angry red. I dragged his coffin behind me, supporting only one end, while the other slid through the worm-infested mud, crushing insect-larvae by the score. The larvae screamed, but very faintly. I imagined that Rowland's dead lips were speaking to me as we went, mocking my slowness.

"Trains of thought need tracks," he told me. "Where are your tracks now, Peter? You'll never get to where you need to be at this rate."

"For the love of God, Rowland!" I complained. I felt thirsty.

That was bad enough, but, after I had immured my one and only friend in a vault behind a great metal door, I remained anchored to the spot, listening for an eternity, waiting for the sounds that I knew would come—the sound of the body risen from its rest, its fingers tapping and scratching at the door, the sound of its heart, beating once again more powerfully than before.

Inevitably—probably, there was no real lapse of time, but simply an aching false consciousness of time passed—the sounds began. The heartbeat taunted my soul with echoes of dread and anguish, which reverberated in my being until I felt myself literally *driven* insane, and howled at myself in the fury of my hallucination: "Madman! Madman! Madman!"

Then I woke in a cold sweat, feeling exceedingly thirsty.

And I heard, outside the door of my chamber, a faint tapping and scratching.

For a moment, I convinced myself that I was still asleep, and struggled manfully to wake. Then I could deny my senses no longer, and knew that the sound was real.

I dragged myself from my bed, feeling very heavy, as if my body required an agony of effort in order to move at all. I stumbled to the door, and opened it, at first by the merest crack and then—in consequence of what I saw—much wider.

There in the faintly-lit corridor, prostrate at my feet, one hand still groping for the door, was what seemed to be a teenage girl.

I knew, of course, that she was not human. How many human

genes were in her—Magdalen Usher's genes, taken from the tissue-cultures that had outlived their source—I could not guess, but I knew that she was a sham, a phantasm, no more human than the maggots that would soon consume Rowland Usher's body…and one day, no doubt, my own.

She didn't look like Magdalen, as I remembered my one and only true love from her teenage years. She didn't look fully or convincingly human, even in the dim light of the corridor. But she was, as Rowland had promised, beautiful. Hers was not the beauty of a butterfly, or a dragonfly, or a colored beetle; it was no kind of beauty that any species of insect had ever manifested before, and it was not, strictly speaking, human beauty—but she *was* beautiful, in a way of her own that seemed poignant and pathetic. She was the kind of creature, undoubtedly, that a human might love…if not, perhaps, a human like me. To me, she was a pitiful creature, and it was pity that moved me to respond to her presence. I remembered what Rowland had said about such creatures not living long

Some insect imagoes, I knew, emerge from their pupae without digestive systems, unable to nourish themselves; they exist only to exchange genes in the physiological ritual of sexual intercourse, and then to die. These creatures of Rowland's did not even have reproductive organs inside them…yet. They existed neither to eat nor to breed, being equipped only with the very minimum of a behavioral repertoire, in order to serve their maker's transitory purpose. That purpose still had a long way to go before it would be properly focused. For now, Rowland's race of New Eves existed purely and simply to assist him in the work of their continued improvement, the ambition of their ultimate perfection. For now, they were merely rough sketches of their ultimate descendants, with tiny random tumors in their unnecessarily voluminous chitinous skulls, which had not yet found the trick of becoming embryonic brains, let alone of actually thinking.

And yet, when I took the pitiful creature in my arms, she was able to cling to me and caress me, to soothe as well as to be soothed. That might have been the entirety of her emotional existence, but it was not negligible. Like a mayfly, she had been born with only a short time to live, innocent and ignorant of time, space and the world at large. Her universe was the House of Usher, and her journey of exploration along the spiral corridor had been the only one she would ever make.

I could only hope that she was passing her brief existence in a kind of bliss, and that I was helping to sustain that absence of terror, expectation and desire.

I was fully awake now, and although I had been startled and a little appalled, I was able to react in a rational manner. I picked the poor creature up and carried her to my bed, where I stroked her, gently

She died before morning.

When I had got dressed, I consulted the map I had decanted on to my handset, and carried her body down the caverns deep underground. They were, indeed, a long way down, but they were still within the living walls of the growing manse, in whose nooks and crannies the free-living maggots pupated.

Down there I saw rank after rank of grey pupae, shaped like the sarcophagi in which the Egyptians entombed their mummi-fied dead. I watched the hatching of a few of the humanoid ephemerae, and studied the phases of their brief life-cycle by inspecting individuals of different ages.

They clustered around me—not driven by curiosity or the hope of caresses, in my judgment, but simply by some instinct of gregariousness. They probably could not tell that I was not one of them, in spite of my stature, age and sex. They had beautiful eyes—eyes, Rowland had told me, had been easy to fake—but they had no idea what they were seeing. They were not blind, but they were not conscious either, so the sensory information they collected either vanished into a void or deployed its effects at a far more basic level than consciousness, or even emotion.

They did not need me to stay with them—those aspects of Rowland's work that had demanded continual and relentless attention were concerned with their further evolution, not their mundane lives—but I did stay with them, for most of the morning. I found their presence comforting.

It was not until Rosalind called me and told me that her flight had landed, and that she was on her way to board a chartered boat, that I went back up to the top of the house, to see Adam and Eve. The three of us grieved for a while. Once the distant post-mortem had been completed, Eve had washed the body and replaced the unclean bedding. The body had been arranged in a resting position. Decay had not yet made measurable progress; that part of the house was sterile.

I read the autopsy results. Rowland had died of a cerebral hemorrhage, apparently occasioned by an anomalous interaction between Aether—the official report gave the full chemical name and formula rather than the familiar term—and a cluster of transformed cells in a localized area of the cerebrum.

The report did not say so, but I knew that the area in question was the one associated with rational and scientific thought... except, of course, that, like genes, brain-cells never do just *one thing*. You can't enhance one propensity without affecting others. Nature is the Mother of improvisation; there's always a trade-off on the road of least resistance, and even when you get what you wanted, you get screwed.

Adam asked me what would happen, now. He meant to him and Eve. I told him that I didn't know, yet—that I would have to talk to Rosalind before making any firm decisions—but that he need have no fear. For as long as he and Eve were prepared to tend to the house, they would be paid to do so. If they no longer wanted to do it, they would be given generous assistance to settle elsewhere.

Adam told me that he didn't want to leave the house. Eve agreed with him. It was their home, their refuge.

Adam and I went down to meet Rosalind's boat when it approached the harbor. She wasn't alone, of course; she had brought four men with her—all drones, I could not help thinking, although I knew that they wouldn't be idle, and I recognized one of them as her petty Saint Peter, who had let me in but wouldn't let me out again while manning the gates of Eden. She left the hirelings to follow orders without direct supervision, though, when she accompanied me to inspect the body of her only son. She didn't touch the body. She simply stood and looked at it, sorrowfully.

"You expected this," I said, accusatively. "You knew something like this was going to happen."

"No I didn't, Peter," she said, flatly. "I feared that it might—but I sent you here in the hope that you might somehow be able to prevent it from happening. It's not your fault that you couldn't. If anyone is at fault, it's me, because I couldn't."

"You should have told me exactly how Magdalen died."

"How could I, Peter? How could I, when I don't even know myself? I know that she poisoned herself, by taking Aether. I tried to stop her, to substitute something more subtle, but she was mirroring what Rowland was doing. She knew that she didn't need to—that he had given her a placebo instead of the loaded vectors—but she couldn't help it. Whatever was driving her was operating below the level of consciousness, immune to any effort of will that she or I could make. I've done my damnedest to figure out the chemistry of such effects—to figure out how subconscious psychtotropics actually work—but even the resources of the Hive couldn't solve the problem in time to help her.

"What was I supposed to tell you, Peter—that she was killed by the placebo effect? I told you what I could: that she was poisoned, that it probably wasn't an accident, and that it definitely wasn't murder. I wasn't even certain of that...but I was worried about Rowland. I thought his arrogance might save him—that even though Magdalen's mirroring of his symptoms had killed her, he might simply be too self-satisfied to surrender to mortality in the same way—but I was wrong about that. I also hoped that your presence might help him, even though it couldn't have helped Magdalen, because you were his friend. That didn't work out either. It's not your fault that it didn't, though, any more than it's his."

It was grief talking. Not that she wasn't telling the truth, but she wouldn't have gone on at such length if she hadn't just suffered the double blow of losing her twins. She certainly wouldn't have framed so many of her comments as questions. If she'd been herself—the Queen Bee—she'd just have given me the facts...but the Queen Bee was just an act. The Queen Bee was a pose she'd learned to strike, in order to compensate for the side-effects of her scientific genius, the forcefulness of her rational objectivity.

"Rowland blamed himself for Magdalen's death," I told her.

"Of course he did," Rosalind retorted. "We all blamed ourselves, reveling in our supposed guilt, masochistic idiots that we are."

She didn't mean that we were idiots who just happened to have a masochistic streak. She meant that the mocking masochism that sometimes welled up from beneath the conscious levels of our minds—from beneath our science—made idiocy of our genius, in a spirit of objective irony.

"Rowland must have known about the danger," I told her. "He must have taken scans, even if he didn't transmit them for analysis by anyone else—but he was in denial. Even though he was in a hurry to give me the keys to his secret, he was still in denial. It wasn't suicide, but there was a certain amount of contributory negligence involved. I came too late. A year ago, perhaps even six months, I might have been able to make a difference...but I left it too late."

"*He* left it too late," Rosalind said. "He could have invited you at any time, and you'd have come—like a shot. You had to wait for an excuse to demand an invitation—for Magdalen to die."

"He left me the house, you know—he wants me to continue his work."

"I know. I knew before I asked you to come. He couldn't keep *that* a secret, and didn't even try."

"Do you intend to challenge the will?"

Rosalind fixed me with her sky-blue eyes, but she didn't attempt to reach out to me. "Why would I do that?" she said. "He was perfectly sane when he made the will, wasn't he?"

I didn't answer that, but she took my silence for assent.

"The Hive doesn't need his money," she went on, "and as for his work…if he was prepared to trust you with it, so am I. You needn't cut yourself off the way he did though. If you want our collaboration, our help…or merely someone to talk to, who understands…."

Again, I said nothing, but this time, she took it as evidence of doubt.

"I *do* understand," she told me. "They didn't think I could, either of them—but I'm their mother. I understood them far better than they knew, far better than they hoped."

I didn't contradict her.

"What are you going to do?" she asked.

To start with, I took her into the underworld, so that she could see with her own eyes what Rowland had wrought, and what it was that he wanted me to continue on his behalf. I told him what he had said to me before he died, including his Romantic flight of fancy.

"They're beautiful," she said, of the ephemerae. They clustered round the two of us, reaching out to us and touching us. I was slightly surprised to see that Rosalind didn't seem to mind their touch at all, and certainly didn't flinch from it. She looked into their empty eyes frankly. Nor was that part of her Queen Bee pose; she really didn't mind. Perhaps, I thought, we had more in common than I'd previously imagined.

"They're modeled on Magdalen," I told her.

"I can see that," she said. "What other model could they possibly have used? Did you expect me to be horrified, Peter? I'm a scientist, like you. Are *you* horrified?"

"No," I admitted—but I was still surprised at myself.

"So what are you going to do?" she asked, again. I saw that, in her turn, she was reaching out to the ephemerae, as I was, and returning their unthinking caresses.

"I don't know," I confessed. "I have my own work, my own life, in Lancaster."

"Do you?" she countered. "What happened when the word got around the university that you were coming out here?"

"People started ringing up to beg me to bring them with me...have you been bugging my phone?"

"Of course not. They rang me too, begging me to intercede on their behalf—I didn't return the calls, obviously. If you need help, there won't be any lack of it. I'll send you a couple of my daughters if you like—but you mustn't fall in love with any of them; there wouldn't be any future in it." She didn't realize how insulting the final comment was.

"Do you *want* me to carry on where Rowland left off?" I asked, slightly incredulously.

"What *I* want doesn't come into it," she said. "That's what *he* wanted. The question I asked, if you need me to repeat it, was what *you* want to do."

"I don't know," I repeated.

"What you need to remember, Peter," she said, "is that if our fundamental impulses are generated somewhere in the dark depths of the brain, beyond the reach of consciousness and rational planning, ever vulnerable to psychotropic agents of which we have no knowledge, let alone understanding, then it's our manifest duty to fight them, to find a way to conquer them and subject them to the empire of reason. However hard it is, we need to exert all the force that consciousness and science can muster. We can't let Mother Nature win. If we can't defeat her in ourselves, we owe it to those who come after us to make sure that they're better armed than we are, so that they have a better chance of succeeding where we failed. That's what being human ought to be about."

"Not everyone would agree with you about that," I said.

"Not everyone," she agreed. "But you do, Peter, don't you?"

I did. In spite of all the faults that my flesh was heir to, I could, and I did.

EPILOGUE

It was very rare that the ephemerae emerged from pupation in isolation. Usually, there were at least half a dozen alive at any one time. By virtue of that fact, they could respond to their innate behavioral drive in flocking together and fondling one another, achieving the meager fulfillment of which they were capable easily, comfortably and—by their own peculiar standards—naturally.

Whenever I had to leave Rowland's house temporarily, to collect my algal specimens, I was sorry to leave the ephemerae behind, even for a matter of hours, because I had grown fond of them, in my fashion. It was in their chamber that Rosalind and I buried Rowland Usher, and I couldn't help feeling that it was unfortunate that his beloved Magdalen hadn't been buried there alongside him. I knew that the brother and sister would have wished to rest side by side. I felt, however—in spite of Rosalind's curt and contemptuous dismissal, when I was unwise enough to confess it to her—that Magdalen really was there in spirit, still haunting the house with her benign and loving presence. For as long as I remained faithful to her memory, I thought, she would never desert me. Magdalen had not been able to love me as I loved her, but she had always been kind.

We had left Rowland lightly coffined, as he had wished, so that his decaying flesh might be absorbed, in due course, by the scavenging cells of the house, thus becoming a part of her ever-extending body, dissipated within her maternal flesh, united with her in substance whether or not any kind of spiritual union were really possible.

I came to love the house, although I never thought to her as a substitute for the mother I had never had, and certainly never referred to her, even in the privacy of my flippant imagination, as Rosalind II.

I didn't have to give up teaching; I invited several of the research students to join me, at least on a temporary basis, and they jumped at the chance. Adam and Eve also became my pupils in genetics and many other braches of science, because they too wanted to do their utmost to perpetuate Rowland's legacy. We soon had the beginnings of a true colony, though not a hive in any accurate metaphorical sense.

Whenever I did venture out of the house, and found myself in the full glare of the tropical sun, I had to wrinkle my nose against the stench of the swamp, for I had become used to breathing clean and sterile air and feared that the complex reek might be concealing some of Mother Nature's insidious olfactory psycho-tropics. The sky always seemed very blue, its light wild and abandoned, and my eyes ached for the gentle roseate glow of the house's bioluminescence. I always took great pride, however, in looked back at the astonishing edifice from a distance, watching her walls gleaming and sparkling as if encrusted with precious gems, and savoring the objective aesthetics of her soft-ened shape, which I liked to fancy as a surreal hand reaching upwards, as if to touch infinity with molten fingers.

She was perfectly lovely.

The fictitious House of Usher—a shameful allegory of the disturbed psyche—was burst asunder by the forces of its own innate decay and swallowed up by dark and unforgiving waters. In stark contrast, Rowland's House of Usher still stands, soaring proudly above the tattered canopy of the twisted trees. It is still growing, and although it stands today in a noisome swamp, there will come a time, even if I have long been buried along-side my friend and absorbed into its flesh as nourishment, when it has purified the lakes and the islands, absorbing their apparent stagnancy into its own manifest vitality.

I cannot claim originality for that thought—it's yet another unashamed quotation. In one of the notes he appended to his data discs, Rowland explicitly contrasted his house with Poe's imaginary one, damning the fictitious original as a typical product of the Romantic imagination and what he considered to be its myriad demonic afflictions. His own house, by contrast, he claimed as a personification of the nascent zeitgeist of the twenty-second century, and of the third millennium: a spirit perhaps best summed up by the reminder that Rosalind gave me, in helping me to make up my mind as to what I intended to do, of the ideal thrust of human duty.

I no longer think of myself as Peter Bell, and certainly not as Peter Bell the Third. I think of myself as Rowland's rock and loyal apostle, with no need of any surname.

Rosalind held a memorial service for Rowland in Eden, a few days after her return to England. Professor Crowthorne was there. He probably hoped and expected to see me, but I was absent—with Rosalind's permission and understanding.

I had work to do. I still have.

ABOUT THE AUTHOR

Brian Stableford was born in Yorkshire in 1948. He taught at the University of Reading for several years, but is now a full-time writer. He has written many science-fiction and fantasy novels, including *The Empire of Fear*, *The Werewolves of London*, *Year Zero*, *The Curse of the Coral Bride*, *The Stones of Camelot*, and *Prelude to Eternity*. Collections of his short stories include a long series of *Tales of the Biotech Revolution*, and such idiosyncratic items as *Sheena and Other Gothic Tales* and *The Innsmouth Heritage and Other Sequels*. He has written numerous nonfiction books, including *Scientific Romance in Britain, 1890-1950*; *Glorious Perversity: The Decline and Fall of Literary Decadence*; *Science Fact and Science Fiction: An Encyclopedia*; and *The Devil's Party: A Brief History of Satanic Abuse*. He has contributed hundreds of biographical and critical articles to reference books, and has also translated numerous novels from the French language, including books by Paul Féval, Albert Robida, Maurice Renard, and J. H. Rosny the Elder.